Riley

By

Ronna M. Bacon

Deuteronomy 31:6 Be strong and of a good courage, fear not, nor be afraid of them: for the LORD your God, he it is that does go with you; he will not fail you, nor forsake you.

Psalm 34:7 The angel of the Lord encamps around those who fear Him, and rescues them.

Table of Contents

Rubbing his hand along the worn and soft cedar railing on the porch outside of a tired general store, Riley Ransome sighed to himself. He had run away from life, he decided, just to try and get a fresh perspective. What his brother, Richard, had gone through when he was forced to marry his wife, Raleigh, had shaken Riley deeply. The danger that his brother and his bride had gone through had only compounded the restlessness that Riley was undergoing. He knew that Richard and Raleigh were deeply in love but it still left him wondering if he would ever find that kind of love.

Riley stared off into the distance, not seeing the strands of trees that surrounded the store or the unkempt appearance close by, the uncut grass, the untrimmed shrubs, and the general lack of care that the store owner didn't seem to worry about. He turned at last, his feet carrying him across the soft, creaking planks on the porch. Riley drew in a deep breath, not sure if the porch was stable enough to hold him. His hand reached for the latch on the old-style screen door, drawing it towards him before he entered the dimly lit building. Blinking, Riley felt his eyes adjusting to the light before he headed for what appeared to be a diner section. He desperately needed a cup of coffee. He had been on the road since early that morning, driving away from his home on the shores of Lake Erie into the central portion of the province of Ontario, not really that far from home but far enough that he could feel nameless to those around him. And that was what he wanted. Riley just didn't realize that he had been followed, the men following him meaning him harm.

Nodding at the lady who approached him, Riley drew in a deep breath. She was a beautiful lady with golden curls and violet eyes, not whom he would have expected to find in such a decrepit building but it was what it was. He wasn't planning on sticking around long enough to find out her history. He turned as he waited for his coffee to be made, not hearing the rough tones of a man who had approached, shoving the lady aside and brusquely ordered her away and back to where she had been.

Sipping at his coffee, Riley wandered the store, frowning at the limited amount of groceries and other items that were available. He shook his head, dizziness hitting for a moment. His hand went to the dark brown curls that he had cropped a little longer than normal before he rubbed at his amber eyes. He had no idea why he felt dizzy. He hadn't been sick or taken anything that would affect his ability to function.

The lady watched him closely, knowing what was happening and unable to prevent it. She shot a look at the gruff and evil man who stood near her, knowing that he would prevent her from helping the man who had appeared without warning. Rayleen Randell was a captive of his and had long struggled to escape. Any attempt on her part had been dealt with in no uncertain terms of cruelty and abuse. Rayleen sighed to herself even as she prayed for the man who was now staggering. She knew exactly what her captor had done. He had drugged the younger man and would not let him escape his cruelty.

Riley's hand rested against a shaky shelf, not feeling the vibration of the wood as he leaned hard against it. The dizziness was growing stronger. He turned to ask for help but didn't make it all the way around before he collapsed, his body hitting hard on the worn wooden and gray floor. He didn't move other than for a slight raising of his head before it dropped back onto his outstretched arm.

The man gave an evil chortle before he was calling on his minions for help. The two men raised Riley to his feet and then almost dragged him from the building, Riley's feet barely able to make a move, tangling over one another and causing him to stumble as he tried to operate them.

Dragged outside of the store and towards another rundown building, Riley was unable to function or even understand that something was going on and that he no longer was a free man. He didn't hear the words that were hammering at him, that he was no longer a free man and that he would work for the store owner in his criminal activities. Dropped to the damp earthen floor of the shack, Riley didn't move. He didn't hear the door close and the lock clicking into place. His head raised slightly for a moment before it dropped onto his outstretched arm and he lost consciousness, dropping down into that well of darkness that seemed to have no bottom.

Night came and still Riley had not moved. The man had been back to stand over him, gloating. He had searched for Riley's identification, staring at him and then at Riley. He knew Riley's brother and hated him.

He just would not articulate to anyone why. He stomped away, the door closed and locked behind him.

Rayleen stood at the window in the shabby room that she was allowed in inhabit. She had no real comforts, nothing that made it feel as if it were her home. She was a prisoner of the man as well, having been kept captive by him for a number of months. Rayleen worried about her family. She knew that they would have been looking for her and not finding her. She was not near her hometown of Elmton. Rayleen had been kidnapped from her work as a wildlife technician one day and taken to that forsaken village. She had attempted to escape many times but was never successful. Rayleen prayed daily for a way to escape, to flee from the man who gloated over having her in his control, but had had to accept the fact that for the moment, she was not able to escape. Her prayer had been for peace and protection. God had granted her that. But with this young man now in the clutches of the store owner? Rayleen was determined to find a way to escape and to help him escape as well. She just didn't know how that would happen but her determination would make that. She sensed a presence in the room with her, an angel sent by God to protect her. Rayleen had caught glimpses of the angel standing in front of the door every night, preventing anyone from entering.

Two days passed this way. Rayleen was forced to work in the store, despite the fact that it was almost always empty. She was kept under strict observation. The store owner knew that she would attempt to escape and he wouldn't let that happen. He had plans for her and those plans now included Riley.

—

Riley roused at last, the drugs leaving his body. He sat up, his arms draped over his upraised knees. He looked around, frowning as his vision cleared. He had no idea where he was or why. On his feet, Riley searched the ramshackle shack, looking for a way out. Hearing a noise at the door, Riley backed away until he felt the wall behind him. He leaned against it, his eyes on the man who entered the shack, silence on his lips, and a shuttered look to his face.

"So, you're on your feet." Fred Logan stared at Riley. "You're not going anywhere. You're going to be working for me." Logan turned and left, an evil laugh echoing in the shack even as the lock clicking shut sounded loud around Riley.

Riley stared at the door before his head dropped. He had no idea who that man was but he had no intentions of working for him. He frowned as he remembered the beautiful lady in the store, around his age, he thought. He had to get free from this building and then free her. Riley had no idea if his truck was still there or if it had disappeared. It didn't matter. He was versed enough in survival techniques in the wild to survive. And survive he would. God had laid that distinctly on his heart. He was there for Riley and would guide him.

Late that night, Riley felt for the door, working away at the soft, rotten wood that made up the door frame. He snorted to himself, wondering how that man thought a rotten, ramshackle building would hold anyone. He cautiously shoved the door open and then shut, making it seem that the lock was still in place. Riley's feet were picked up and set down quietly as he moved towards the living quarters of the store. He had no idea where to find the lady but he was determined to do that and free her.

Glimpsing up, he caught the faintness of a white face at a window and approached it. Raising the window quietly, Rayleen stared at Riley before she was grabbing for her backpack that held bottles of water and some dried food, things that she had taken that day from the store. She would be severely punished if she remained, she knew. The store owner would do that.

Reaching for the lady, Riley simply lifted her through the window and then pulled the window down. He frowned as he saw a figure standing inside, not moving, before he reached for the lady's hand and ran. He looked for his truck, not seeing it. That was about what Riley had expected.

Their feet were picked up and set down as quietly as they could as Riley and Rayleen ran for the trees, her hand tight in his. Riley was not letting her go. It seemed hours before he paused, staring behind him before he stared down at the lady beside him. Both were breathing heavily from their run.

"I need to introduce myself. I'm Riley Ransome. And you would be?" Riley's grin showed briefly in the moonlight.

"Me? I'm Rayleen Randell." She frowned at him. "You look familiar."

"You as well. Come on. We need to keep moving. I have no idea who that man is or what he wants, but he is evil." Riley looked down at her as she grimaced. "Rayleen? May I call you that?"

"You can. And he is evil. You're not the first one that he has imprisoned in this way. He did that to me. He kidnapped me from where I was working just outside of Elmton. I've been imprisoned here for months."

Riley paused for a moment, his mind tracing back on what his friend, Bill Butler, a police detective, had mentioned in their Bible study and prayer group not that long before. A lady was missing from Elmton, a lady by the name of Rayleen Randell, and they had no clue as to where she was. God had led Riley to her and it was up to him and God to get her back to her family.

"I'll get you home, Rayleen. We're from the same town." He frowned at her. "I've seen you around church."

Rayleen frowned up at him before nodding.

"Your brother? He has that security team." Rayleen was confident in her words.

"He does. And that team will work towards finding out why you were taken and bringing whoever it was to justice."

Chapter 2

Reaching once more for Rayleen's hand, Riley walked forward, his head turning as he listened for anyone following them or for anything that would mean harm to them. He wasn't hearing anything but that didn't mean danger was not out there. Riley had learned from his brother just how dangerous life could be, and he didn't want to face that. Only thing was, he already had.

"What's that man's problem?" Riley's question was low-voiced but still firm. "What did he want with you?"

Rayleen studied the tall, handsome man who was holding her hand, something that she never did, allow a man to hold her hand. She thought through his question and then shrugged.

"I have no idea. I was just out there doing my work as a wildlife technician one day, studying the beavers in the area, when two men approached me. I had no chance to run. They bound my hands and then forced me to leave what I was working with and just walked away from me. I struggled to escape but couldn't. They were just too strong for me. I was shoved into a vehicle and they took off. The store where you found me? That's where I ended up, much against my will. I tried numerous times to escape but was never successful. I received beatings and deprivation of food and sleep because of that. How do you explain that to anyone?"

"I understand, Rayleen, better than you think. My brother's security team? All of them faced danger and kidnappings with their now spouses. Even my brother. His wife? They were forced to marry or Raleigh would have been killed in front of him. How do you explain that away?" Anger caused Riley's words to have a bite to them, not directed at Rayleen but at what Richard and his team had faced.

Rayleen stopped moving forward, her hand tugging at Riley to stop. She could hear the sounds of the night around them, sounds of nature that brought comfort to her. For now, there were no sounds of anything human other than the two of them.

"Is that the truth, Riley?" She waited patiently for Riley to finally nod. "You would never know it. They are so much in love. God was there for them and brought them through it all. He'll bring us out of this, whatever it is. I have no idea what he wanted from me. He's an evil, evil man. That store? It's a front for his criminal activities. There is a small village not too far from it but it only houses his men and their women. I can't call them ladies. They aren't that."

"I see." Riley tugged at Rayleen to get her moving again. "I suspect then that he'll be after us as soon as he knows that we're gone. Does he have dogs?"

"Dogs?" Rayleen was puzzled at the question. "Why would you wonder if he had dogs?"

"Rayleen? Dogs? Tracking? Hound dogs that won't give up until they find us?" Riley was highly worried about that. This was hunting country. If it was hunting country, then that man likely had hound dogs that would follow them. It would be difficult for them to stay ahead of the hunt if that was the case.

Rayleen's face paled as she understood the ramifications of what Riley had asked. She shuddered at the thought of being back in that man's hands. They would not survive, of that she was convinced.

"He does. I heard him boasting about how they can track. Riley? How do we get out of here and away from him? We're out in the middle of nowhere!" Her voice was riddled with fear.

"I know that we are." Riley paused, making Rayleen sit for a moment on a fallen tree trunk. He sat beside her, reaching for her hand again as he prayed for them and begged God to protect them and to bring them to safety. When he was finished, he hesitated before he pulled out his phone. He had service, wonder of wonders, he thought, and sent a quick text off to Richard, simply stating approximately where he was and that he and the lady with him needed help. He also asked Richard to contact Bill, that he had found Rayleen Randell. "I just reached out to my brother. He'll track me. We have that ability on our phones. It will take him a few hours to reach here. We need to find somewhere we can be safe until he reaches us."

"I have no idea where that would be." Rayleen's head dropped. She was exhausted beyond what she had ever been. Being brought away from that man had loosened the hard and tight grip that she had had on her emotions. Tears blinded her for a moment. Rayleen heard an exclamation from Riley before he had wrapped her into his arms and was praying for her. She had not had that for a long time. She was estranged from her parents and her brother and had not heard from them for a number of years.

"We'll make it out safely, Rayleen. And we'll find out why this happened. I doubt that he is the man in charge of this. Elmton is too far from here for him to have known about you." Riley was on his feet, his hand tight on Rayleen's, as he moved them forward. Fatigue dogged both of them as they walked, their feet stumbling at times. "Can I ask you something, Rayleen?"

Rayleen shrugged, not sure what Riley was meaning.

"Of course. What would you like to know about my life?" Riley's words were somewhat bitter. She had no friends in Elmton and lived a lonely solitary life.

"When I shut the window to the room you were held in, I saw a form inside. You were the only one there, correct?" Riley waited patiently for her to speak. Patience was something that he shared with Richard. Both men had the ability to ask a question and then wait for an answer, whether it came or not at the time.

"There was. Every night, I saw a form standing in front of the door. It was an angel sent by God to protect me. I have no doubt about that." Rayleen sighed. "And you don't believe me."

"I do. I have heard of that. A friend's wife? An angel got her grandmother away from the village where they lived and then was there to help her escape. She's not the first one that I have heard of that. God provides us with guardian angels. He gives his angels charge to look after us and protect us. That is what happened with you."

Rayleen looked up at him, tears once more blinding her eyes.

"You believe that, don't you? That's what I have always believed but I didn't think it was possible. I guess it is."

"It is highly likely and more than probable." Riley was not listening to his words, missing the smile that crossed Rayleen's face. "God does protect us. He hides us in the cleft of the rock and He covers us with His hands. I have seen that happen more than once." Riley paused for a moment to look behind him. There was silence and no sound of anything human related. But he knew that would change.

The chiming of his phone startled Rayleen and she gave a small scream, a hand clapped over her mouth to cover that. Her eyes were huge as she watched Riley pull out his phone and then smile.

"It's Richard. He's on his way with his team and with Bill and Jason as well. Bill and Jason are police officers. He's meeting us about an hour from here, he says. We just need to keep walking west." He grinned at the snort that Rayleen gave, not expecting that from her.

"And just how do we know which is west?" Rayleen was getting combative the more tired that she grew. She sighed, opened her mouth to apologize, and then snapped it closed as Riley shook his head.

"We're walking west now. We just have to keep moving. And we will. God will provide the strength that we need." Riley was confident in that. He knew and trusted God.

Chapter 3

Riley just kept trudging forward, his steps becoming slower and slower as the moments passed. He didn't know if he would make it to where he needed to be without collapsing. The fear and stress that was driving him was draining his strength and ability to set one foot ahead of the other. Riley turned to watch Rayleen, seeing the struggle that she was having. He sighed. This was not how his week away was to have been. He had planned on finding a nice campsite and just spending time refreshing himself with his Heavenly Father. Riley felt that he desperately needed that time. Only, it hadn't happened. He had come to the rescue of a beautiful lady and in no uncertain terms would he abandon her.

Dropping to the ground, Rayleen felt her hand slipping away from Riley as her senses dimmed. She collapsed totally, not hearing the sounds of the awakening day critters and creatures. Riley dropped to his knees, shaking her to awaken her with no success. He looked up to where he could see the brightening sky and prayed. He didn't know if he had the strength to carry her any further. Glancing at his watch, Riley shook his head. They still had a ways to go and he didn't think that they would make it. His phone was out as he sent a text to Richard and then pocketed it once more.

Riley stared down at the lady in front of him, trying to determine how to proceed. He rose and then bent to gather Rayleen into his arms. Her arms came around his neck as she settled against him. He studied her, a crack growing in the bonds around his heart. He didn't want to let her go, ever, but that was exactly what he knew would happen. Riley and Rayleen would see each other around town or around church but would have gone their separate ways. Little did he know that this would not be happening.

Setting one foot ahead of the other, Riley continued to move forward, albeit very slowly. He tripped on occasion, fatigue weighting down his feet. He finally had to stop and sit, Rayleen gathered close to him. His head went back against the tree that he was leant against. His eyes closed as he slept, unable to stay awake long enough to watch for danger. And danger was approaching. Their escape had been discovered early in the morning, leaving the man enraged. The dogs were called out and even now were closing in on the couple.

Richard paused beside the SUV that he had just exited. His eyes raised to the lightening sky as he prayed for his brother and the lady whom he seemed to be with. He was afraid, more afraid for his brother than he had ever been. Richard prayed that Riley was not off on an adventure such as he had experienced but he feared that was exactly what was happening. He turned as he felt a hand on his shoulder.

Stephen, Naomi, and Silver from his team stood around him, watching for any danger. Bill and Jason, two police detectives and friends, watched as well, waiting for Richard to make a move. Timothy, the remaining member of his team, watched from where he sat behind the wheel of one of the SUV's. He would not be going anywhere. Nollan, Naomi's husband, was behind the wheel of the other SUV, watching as well. He was afraid for his wife but understood that she was highly trained as were all of the members of her security team. Richard would have it no other way.

Richard looked around before his head was bowed to pray for them as they moved in. He had read his brother's last text message and frowned at it. Riley was in trouble and in danger and he had to move in to find him. He just didn't know if they would in time.

Moving forward with confidence that he was on the right track, Richard led the group towards his brother. He could hear the faint baying of hound dogs in the distance and frowned even deeper. This was not what he had wanted to hear.

Silver moved up to walk beside Richard, her head turning as she looked for any danger that might appear.

"Those are dogs that we hear, Richard. Are they tracking Riley?" She was afraid for the man she considered a brother.

"I would suspect so. And that means we need to find him and find him fast." Richard's steps slowed as he frowned even deeper before he was moving ahead almost on a run, confident in his team and friends that they were still alert for danger.

Dropping to his knees beside Riley, Richard shook his brother to try and awaken him. It succeeded to some degree.

"Richard? What? Where am I?" Riley blinked at his brother, not sure where he was at the moment. "Why are you here?"

"Come on, Ry. On your feet." Richard waited as Stephen gathered Rayleen up from Riley's arms and headed back towards the vehicles before he drew Riley up. With one of Riley's arms around his shoulders, he wrapped one of his around his brother and nodded at Bill and Jason. "Let's get out of here. Those dogs are getting closer."

Bill had been studying the tracks from the couple and then turned back to Richard.

"I think that you are correct, Richard. They're tracking Riley and Rayleen. Let's move. I don't want a confrontation out here. We're out of our town and would have to answer to another force. We don't need that." Bill turned and walked rapidly after the others, sharing a look with Jason, who was in agreement with his fellow detective.

Stephen slid Rayleen onto one of the seats, fastening her in. He turned as he heard Riley protesting that there was a lady that he needed to rescue and kept trying to turn and go back for her. Richard's voice could be heard telling his brother that the lady was safe and would he just get in the vehicle? Shoving Riley in at last, Richard landed on the front passenger seat, watching as the others sorted themselves out.

Riley shook his head, the fog of fatigue still too strong for him to realize that they were safe. He turned slightly to see Rayleen beside him. An arm came out to wrap around her and draw her close to him, preventing Stephen, the paramedic on the team, from doing a proper assessment.

Stephen sat back, watching Riley, frowning at the other man. This is not how Riley treated the ladies. Both the brothers had been very careful in their approach to any of the ladies, not wanting to leave an impression that they were interested in any of them without cause.

"Riley?" Stephen's voice broke Riley's attention to him. "Are you hurt in any way?"

Riley's thought processes were still slow. They could see him trying to think through what Stephen had asked.

"No, I don't think so. I'm just tired. I think that I was drugged a couple of days ago. It took me a day or so to recover. I was kept captive in a ramshackle building. I was able to get out last night and found Rayleen. She's been held captive here since she disappeared. We need to protect her, Richard. How do we do that?" Riley's voice died away as his head dropped onto Rayleen's and he slept. His sentences were choppy and slowly spoken, almost hesitantly. This was totally unlike his normal, firm and concise way of speaking.

Stephen stared at him in shock. This was not the way that Riley normally reacted. He shared a look with Richard, shook his head.

Richard had shifted on his seat as his brother spoke, a frown on his face before he shared a look with Bill who was in the vehicle with them. He shook his head. Richard knew that Bill would be questioning

Riley further and then approaching the police force in the area.

"Let's get them home and then to the hospital to be assessed." Richard bit at his lip, uncertain as to the best course of action. That was unlike him, but then again, this was his brother. Nothing like this had happened to a family member before.

The vehicles had disappeared by the time the man and his minions had appeared. The dogs had tracked the couple to the clearing where the vehicles had sat. He grew angry, loud words spewed at the man, as he strode around, kicking at anything that got in his way. They had walked for hours for nothing. The men with him grew impatient and then just walked away, leaving him on his own. His shouts for them to return fell on deaf ears. They had had enough and just left him there on his own.

The man's phone was out as he demanded one of the men left at the store find him and drive him home. He was already plotting how he could get Riley and Rayleen back in his care. His face grew more evil as the plots became more serious and dangerous for the couple.

Chapter 4

Riley stumbled over his feet as Richard and Bill aided him into the Emergency Department of the local hospital. He had not fully awakened but still kept insisting that there was a lady whom he needed to find. He didn't understand that Rayleen was with him, being carried by Stephen to another examination room.

Slumping back on the stretcher, Riley's eyes closed. He could hear the sounds around him and grew discouraged. He didn't need to be there, he decided. He wanted to rise and find Rayleen, but someone kept him from that. His eyes opened for a moment as Riley searched for the man who had held them captive. He wasn't in the room but Riley suspected that he would appear and soon. There would be no way that he would let Riley and Rayleen live now that they had escaped from him. That caused fear to grow in Riley's heart. He wanted to protect Rayleen. He just didn't know if she would allow him that privilege. And a privilege it would be, Riley decided.

Richard stood where he could monitor his brother but also keep watch on the activity around him. They didn't think that they had been followed but it was entirely possible for that man to reach out to their town of Elmton once more. All of them were puzzled as to why Rayleen had been kidnapped and then held against her will for so long. It also puzzled them why Riley had ended up there. It was off the beaten path and not somewhere that he would normally travel to.

Bill had stayed long enough to ensure that he had the couple's statements before he was away. Jason stayed, just to provide a police presence for them. The medical staff were familiar enough with the two officers not to question why they were there.

Rayleen had roused finally, staring around in terror until she realized that she was safe and that help was there. She slipped away at last from the room, searching for her rescuer. Rayleen stood in the doorway, watching Riley, before she was beside him, a hand on his shoulder. She needed to be with him, just why that was, Rayleen wasn't sure.

Richard watched from near the doorway as Riley roused enough to reach for Rayleen's hand. He shook his head as his brother then slid from the stretcher and with Rayleen's hand tight in his, walked towards him. He frowned at the look on Riley's face, not realizing that it was mimicking the one that had been on his face in the early stages of his and Raleigh's adventures. The difference was that Richard and Raleigh were forced to marry. Riley and Rayleen were still single. Richard turned his head slightly as he heard a sound from beside him.

Naomi and Silver watched the man whom they considered a brother hesitantly walk towards them. This was not Riley, they knew.

"Richard? What did they say about them?" Silver asked the question that the team were wondering about.

"Not a lot. Riley was drugged, from what we can deduce. That is still affecting him to some degree.

And walking all night has not helped. As to Rayleen? No one has said." Richard reached a hand out to steady his brother. "For now, we need to keep them together."

"At your place." Naomi nodded at Riley. "We need to, Riley. You are victims of crime and Bill and Jason will be back around many times to pick your brain about what happened." She grinned at him as he scowled back at her. "You know that from what Richard went through."

"I know. I just don't have to like it." Riley tugged on Rayleen's hand. "I guess we need to go to Richard's then, Rayleen. Do we need to stop at your home?"

Rayleen sighed. This is not what she wanted to have happen but it appeared that God was directing her steps at the moment away from her home.

"I guess." She paused for a moment. "I just don't know if it's safe."

"That's okay, Rayleen. Richard and his team will search it for you." Riley suddenly just wrapped her into a hug. "We've got you."

Rayleen stared up at him, shocked at his actions. It was definitely not what she had expected. The sounds of the busy Emergency ward disappeared and faded for a moment as she study the tall, handsome man who was holding on to her.

"I guess. It's been a couple of months since I was there. I have no idea what the condition of it will be." Rayleen bit at her lip. "I don't need to contact my family. They walked away from me years ago, even my brother.”

“And we will arrange that.” Richard’s hand hit his brother’s back. “Riley, we need to move and get you two somewhere safe until we can assess what we need to do. Out with you.”

Riley nodded, turning Rayleen to walk from the hospital and back to the SUV’s that were waiting for them. He reached for Rayleen’s hand after they were buckled into their seats, his grip just strong enough to steady her and relieve some of the fear that seemed to be growing so quickly within her.

Pulling to a stop outside of a small brick home, Timothy stared at it and then at Richard, who nodded. Both felt something off about the home. There would be no way that they would allow Rayleen into her home until it had been searched.

“Rayleen? May we have your keys?” Richard shifted to watch her, seeing as she sighed and then frowned at him. “You have been away from here for a while. It’s what we do, Rayleen. We look around outside and then go inside. Would your family have been in and out of it?”

Rayleen nodded. They would have been. And what sort of danger had they been in as they did so?

“They would have, Richard. And I don’t know what they would have seen or not seen. They don’t come around a lot. We’re not that close.” Rayleen handed over the keys to her home, frowning at them. “They never took my keys. That’s odd.”

—

Richard paused for a moment, his hand tightening around the keys. Something was definitely off about that.

"It is odd, Rayleen. They obviously didn't expect you to escape. What about your phone?" Richard watched with slight amusement as she stared at him and then pulled a phone from her pocket.

"This phone? The one that needs charging? They didn't take it either." Rayleen's head went down against Riley without her realizing what she had done. "What did I do?"

"You didn't do anything, Rayleen." Timothy looked around at her, watching both Rayleen and Riley. "It's them that's done something. I'm staying put while the other four search. And they will call in Bill or Jason if they need to."

"That's what I'm afraid of. That they'll find something and I have to leave my home." Rayleen's voice and face were sober. They could tell that she was struggling to control her emotions and to tamp down the fear that she felt.

Chapter 5

Watching Richard's team as they worked around her home, Rayleen grew more and more afraid. She had no idea why she had been kidnapped in the first place and then held as she had been. She wanted answers that didn't appear to be coming.

Riley tilted his head to watch the lady sitting so tight to him. He didn't think Rayleen realized that she had been shifting closer and closer to him as the moments passed.

"Rayleen? What do you think they'll find?" Timothy shot a glance back at her before he was once more searching the area around the vehicle. The vehicle had not been turned off, Timothy ready to drive off if necessary.

"I don't know. Just a lot of dust, I hope." Rayleen sighed. "But you think otherwise."

Timothy shrugged. It was entirely possible that there might be something inside her home. And then again, there just might be dust as she suggested.

Richard walked back towards the vehicle, nodding as his team spread out around the house. This was when it could be dangerous for Rayleen, going into her home. Leaning an arm on the top of the open door to the back seat, Richard looked around. He didn't feel anyone watching them and for that he thanked God.

"We've been through your home, Rayleen. We can't tell if anything is out of order. Only you can do that. But it is clean. Would someone have done that?" He waited for her to answer, not sure if she would.

"It's possible. A friend has a key. She might have cleaned." Rayleen drew in a trembling breath. "There isn't anything there that shouldn't be?"

"Not that we can tell. Come on. Let's get you in and out and then to my place. Raleigh will have a meal ready for you and then you two need to sleep. Bill or Jason or even Lily will be around later just to talk with you."

Riley's hand was tight on Rayleen's once more as they walked the front sidewalk to her home. Rayleen was hesitant to enter her home, not sure what she would find. Drawing in a deep breath, she stepped across the threshold into the entryway and stopped. There was just no way that she could go any further. It was as if God had planted a huge wall in front of her.

The men with her frowned at her and then at one another. Riley simply turned Rayleen around and back to the SUV. Richard's phone was in his hand as he paced away from the home.

"Bill? We're at Rayleen's home. She can't go into it any further than just inside the front door. We walked through it and didn't see anything. But your team needs to go through it." Richard could hear Bill's footsteps as he rapidly walked through the department building. "I'm heading off with them. Stephen will wait here with her keys."

"That's what we wondered, wasn't it? That somehow they managed to get into her home. And from what you are describing, I would say that they had." Bill was frustrated. This whole situation with Riley and Rayleen was not making sense. He had reached out to a friend on the police force in that area and asked for any information that he could give. That friend had agreed and would forward what he had. Not that it was a lot. The man hid his activities only too well.

Raleigh watched as Richard and his team walked Riley and Rayleen towards her. She frowned. She knew Rayleen slightly from church and wondered just how she had come into their lives. She looked up. God had done that and God was once more working in lives in ways that they didn't expect or even like. Riley was in danger and that scared Raleigh. She remembered only too well how she and Richard had felt.

Reaching to hug Raleigh, Riley stood back for a moment, assessing her and then assessing Rayleen. He could tell that the ladies had an acquaintance just by their reactions towards one another. A hand on his back shoved him forward and into the house before Richard shut the door and then walked around the perimeter of his property. Silver, Naomi, and Stephen were doing the same, in work mode once more. Nollan had left them at the hospital, heading for work, although he didn't want to be there. He wanted to hear the tale of the adventure that Riley and Rayleen were having. He knew that would come at some point.

Riley walked back towards the kitchen, showered and in clean clothes once more. He sighed. He was exhausted to the point that he could barely function. Raleigh took one look at him and turned him to the living room.

"Sit, Riley. I'll bring in your meal. You need to sleep." She grinned at him as he shook his head. "Rayleen will be down shortly. She's terrified, Riley. How do we help you two?"

Riley shrugged, his eyes on Rayleen as she hesitated before his hand was held out to her. She almost ran towards him, clutching at his hand and then sitting as tight to him as she could as he pulled her down on the couch. He was her lifeline right now, a lifeline that she didn't want to let go of but one that she couldn't really understand. God was working in their lives, providing protection and security at the moment with Richard and his team. She just didn't know where it went from there.

Rayleen's eyes took in the comfortable living room before she looked up at Riley. He was slumped into the corner of the couch, his eyes closed. Exhaustion was written on his face, she could see. Looking around as she heard footsteps, Rayleen frowned at the man who walked towards them.

"Rayleen?" Andrew McBeth, the town police chief, found a seat where he could study the couple. And they were a couple, he had to agree with Raleigh's assessment of them. "What can we do for you?"

"What can you do for me? I'm not sure that I understand." Raleigh's voice was low, barely audible, before her head was down against Riley's shoulder and she slept.

Andrew shook his head, taking with thanks the mug of coffee handed to him. They wouldn't be speaking with either one of the couple at that point.

———

33

Jason was planning on coming around later that day, just to elicit as much more information from them as he could.

"Thanks, Richard. They're not moving from here." Andrew gave a brief smile.

"No, they're not. They need each other." Richard sighed as he took found a seat in his favourite chair. "They're like the rest of us." Andrew and his wife, Phoebe, had shared an adventure just as had many of their friends.

"They are. We need to stop that man but I'm not sure how we can." Andrew was on his feet, heading back to the police detachment. He shook his head. He had not expected Riley to be on a life-changing and dangerous adventure. Andrew paused for a moment to pray for his friend. He was not as close to Riley as he was to Richard but they were friends. It would appear that they would now become better friends.

Chapter 6

Riley was on his feet two hours later, searching for the man who had held them captive. He stood on Richard's back deck, staring at the back of the property, certain that the man had found him. There would be no way that the man would let them live now.

Timothy watched Riley for a moment before he approached him, simply standing shoulder to shoulder with his friend. They were all concerned about their boss' brother, knowing that he was in danger and that the danger would only increase.

"Riley? What more can you tell us?" Timothy spoke at last.

Riley shrugged. He had no idea what he could say. He felt as if the team had picked his brain clean. He shifted on his feet, turning slightly to look at the door behind him. He didn't see the comfortable wicker furniture on the deck or the bright and colourful flowers. Instead, Riley was focused on Rayleen, knowing that they would go their separate ways soon.

"I don't know what more that I can say, Timothy. I didn't really get a look at him or anyone else. There just wasn't time. I saw Rayleen and then took my cup of coffee. Whatever was in it? It took me down quickly."

"And it took a lot to do that." Timothy was frustrated at not having the information that they needed. "God was protecting you, my friend. It could have been a lot worse."

"It could have." Riley hesitated to speak. "I know that it was mentioned, but Rayleen said that a form stood in front of her door each night. I saw the form after I helped her from the room. I am sure that God provided an angel to protect her."

"And He would have. He does that. It's not the first time that we have heard of something like that."

"No, it's not." Riley's hand was out for Rayleen's as she appeared in the doorway, hesitating to approach the two men. "It's okay, love. Timothy is just trying to understand what happened."

"I get that. I don't understand." Rayleen blinked against the setting sun. "I need to call my boss. I am sure that he thinks I abandoned my position."

Naomi had approached them and began to shake her head.

"Not at all, Rayleen. He was around last week, in fact, asking if there was any way that Richard and our team could help find you." Naomi reached to hug Rayleen before she drew her away from Riley.

Rayleen was reluctant to leave the safety that she felt with the man who had walked away with her from her captivity. She turned her head to watch him, seeing something in his eyes that caused her to draw in a deep breath. Rayleen was certain that they would go their separate ways. But she prayed that God would not allow that, that Riley would stay in her life. She had never prayed that way before and wondered that she was.

The ladies from the team as well as the wives had all gathered in the kitchen, working on a meal for them. Rayleen stood for a moment, feeling as if she was an outsider, but she was not allowed to feel like that for long. She was simply drawn into the group. Laughter wafted outside to the men, who all smiled. The team that had been in for training was gone and Richard's team was now free for the evening.

Richard pulled his brother to one side, assessing him carefully.

"Riley? Just how are you doing?" He waited patiently for his brother to gather his thoughts and then speak.

Riley shrugged. He had no idea how he was to feel and stated at much. He saw the men around him nodding before their heads were bowed and they began to pray for both himself and Rayleen. He listened carefully to his brother's prayer, hearing him end with his usual "I love you". Riley had asked Richard about that when he first started saying that. His brother had shrugged and stated that God needed to hear that they loved him.

"I have no idea how to feel." Riley walked away from the group, needing some alone time. He was like that, they all knew. Jason paced beside him, not willing to let him get away without speaking. "Jason? What more do you need to know?"

"I am not sure, Riley. We've gone over your statement. Bill reached out to the force in the area. The store has been abandoned today, from what they said. That means the man is moving in on you in our town. How do we keep you and Rayleen safe? You'll both be at your own homes."

Riley shrugged. He knew that would be the case. He had no answers for Jason.

"Is that right? Then, how do we protect Rayleen? He'll be after her again and this time, she'll disappear for good." Riley turned to study his brother's property, taking in the buildings and the house that had to have been rebuilt after the original one was destroyed by a bomb.

"That I can't tell you, Riley. We don't have the information that we need to find the man or whoever it is that he will have hired. You know how it works, unfortunately." Jason finally walked away, frustrated that he could not solve the mystery surrounding Rayleen. He had spoken at length with her. She had just not been able to provide any further information for him.

Rayleen walked towards Riley, finding him waiting to hug her. She clung to him, an unusual act for the beautiful lady. She did not hug men.

"Okay, love?" Riley's prayer whispered in her ear as he asked that question.

Rayleen shrugged, not wanting to move away from him but knowing that she had to.

"I need to go home, Riley." She drew in a shuddering breath.

"I know you do. Tomorrow is Saturday. We'll get you home tomorrow. For tonight, we'll stay here."

—

He grinned down at her suddenly. "Do you know that we are neighbours?"

Rayleen looked up at him in shock, not sure what to say.

"Neighbours? We are? I didn't know that. I haven't gotten to know my neighbours. I tend to keep to myself."

"We know that you do. We've prayed for you. I live two doors down from you."

"You're the one who mows the lawns for the seniors, aren't you?" Rayleen suddenly gave him a hug. "Not many do that."

"No, they don't. It was how Richard and I were raised. Dad always said that we had to take care of the seniors. It was how God wanted us to be His hands and feet on earth."

Rayleen nodded. That was a good way to express it.

"Can I ask you a question?" She waited until she felt him nod, her head not rising from his chest. "How do we find this man? Jason said he's likely in the area."

"He is. Tomorrow, Richard's team is meeting in the morning, just to get started on an investigation. It's what they do. And we have friends that we can reach out to. In fact, I can guarantee you that they already have been contacted. Richard or one of them would have."

"That's what they do?" Rayleen leaned back to look up at him. "Then, we work it. Raleigh sent me to find you. They have a meal ready."

"And we eat. Then we spend time in prayer." Riley hugged her again before he turned her back to the house, an arm around her. "It's how we do things, Rayleen. You're a part of our group now, did you know that?"

Chapter 7

Early the next morning, Riley was on his feet, wandering through his brother's home to stand outside. He was restless and just wanted to go to his own home. However, he didn't want to leave Rayleen, and that's what would have to happen for him to go home. Riley's head turned slightly as he heard soft footsteps approaching him and then an arm wrapping around his.

Rayleen had found the man who in the night she had conceded she was beginning to love. She had never believed in love at first sight but with Riley, that is exactly what had happened. She would never tell him, not unless he responded that he loved her.

"Riley? Can we go home?" Rayleen's voice was quiet, barely audible in the early morning air.

"We can. Timothy brought my truck around last night. Come on. I'll take you home." Riley reached for her hand and walked towards his truck. He stopped as she pulled back on his hand.

"We can't just walk away from Richard and Raleigh. What will they think?" Rayleen was horrified that Riley was prepared to do just that. Her gaze skittered about as she observed the yard and the buildings and then listened to the early morning sounds of nature.

"Richard's up and watching." Riley nodded towards the house. "He knows we're heading out." Riley's hand went up as he waved at his brother, seeing Richard's wave in return.

"He is? Oh, okay then." Rayleen tugged at Riley's hand this time to walk forward. "This is good bye, I guess, then, Riley. We won't see each other much."

Riley tilted his head to watch her face as he unlocked the truck door and then helped her inside. He drew in a deep breath as he walked around to the driver's side and climbed in.

"It's not good bye, Rayleen. We're neighbours but more importantly, we have shared something dangerous. We can't lose sight of or contact with one another until the detectives have solved it and given us the people and reasons why." Riley gave a quick grin as she frowned at him, thinking how adorable she looked. "I don't want to lose your friendship, Rayleen."

Rayleen thought through his words and then nodded.

"I don't want to lose yours either, Riley. I just thought that we would once we were home again."

"It won't happen, Rayleen. I can guarantee the ladies of the team and the wives will keep in touch with you. We have many friends who have gone through different adventures and they will all want to speak with you. It helps to hear how others coped and how God led and protected each one of them." Riley pulled to a stop in front of his home. "Let's get you home, Rayleen. I want to walk through your house for you before I leave." He gave her no option on that, staring her down.

Rayleen finally nodded. Riley's caring and concern for her was something that she was beginning to accept. She had not really had it in her life and should have.

Riley stood for a moment outside of Rayleen's home, knowing that once he stepped inside, it would change something in their relationship. He just wasn't sure what. He moved in a hesitant manner to step inside, his hand reaching to stop Rayleen. Only he was too late. Rayleen had moved further into the house, a scream wrenched from her as hands grasped at her arms.

Throwing himself towards Rayleen, Riley didn't feel the fists that pommeled at him and then left him in a crumpled heap on the floor. Rayleen lay within feet of him, knocked to the floor and then knocked unconscious. Neither of them heard the men fleeing the house through the back door.

Raising himself slightly as he roused, Riley blinked to clear his vision before his hand was reaching for Rayleen. It rested on her foot before his head dropped back to his arm and he felt nothing or heard nothing.

Three hours later, the older lady who lived in the house between them stepped from her porch, her eyes on Riley's truck. It wasn't parked in his own driveway and that confused her. Walking across her lawn, Georgia Browne looked towards Rayleen's home, a frown on her face, before she walked across that lawn and up the front door. She paused as she saw the door open, something that never happened at that time of day. Georgia had not heard that Rayleen was back home.

Stepping up to the front door, Georgia called for Rayleen, squinting to see inside. She stepped just inside the front door, a scream torn from her as she saw the two bodies. She ran for the neighbour across the street from Rayleen's, barely audible as she stammered out her findings.

The man, John Dodge, held Georgia steady with hands on her upper arms before he was calling for his wife to contact the authorities. He was running for Rayleen's, stopping just as Georgia had inside the front door. He desperately wanted to go further to assess them to assure himself that they were still alive but he knew better.

Andrew watched from the front walk as Bill and Lily stood on the porch. Their attention was on the paramedics as they worked on the couple, assessing them and then readying them for transport to the hospital. He shook his head before he walked away.

Richard stood at the police tape near his brother's truck, worry evident on his face. His team was around as well, their attention on the spectators. They knew many of them as Riley's neighbours. He had been called by Bill, just asking where Riley was. Richard hadn't know at the time that his brother was laying beaten and almost lifeless on the floor inside the house.

Bill turned at last and walked towards Richard, who drew in a deep breath. He didn't like the look on Bill's face. His parents had reached out to him and then headed for the hospital. Richard knew that Raleigh was there. All he could do was pray for his brother and the lady in his life.

"Bill? What can you tell me?" Richard didn't hesitate to ask.

"Riley's been beaten, Richard. We have no information on who yet. And Rayleen was assaulted as well. Both of them are unconscious at the moment. Head on over and find your parents. We're going to be here a while." Bill frowned, pulling his upper lip over his teeth. "When did they come home?"

"When? Around six this morning. I watched them leave. I couldn't stop them. You know that well, Bill. They're adults, capable of making their own decisions, even when those decisions lead them into danger." Richard studied the house and then turned to study what he could see of his brother's. "They were waiting for them."

"From what we can see, they were. Rayleen doesn't have a home security system. I expect that to change." Bill gave a grim smile. "I know your guys will look after that. If not, we have friends who will."

Richard gave a short harsh laugh. They did indeed have friends who would look after that. He was good friend with two other men who had security teams. Any one of those team members would step in and help.

"We do. Call me later. I want to know what you can tell me." Richard walked away, his team gathering with him. "Bill can't say much as yet, guys and ladies. We're heading for Riley and Rayleen. And for now,

—

45

we're their security. Naomi, Silver. You're with Rayleen. Timothy and Stephen, you're with Riley. From what I understand, they are in no shape to complain or protest." Richard worried deeply about the couple before his worry turned to prayer.

—

Chapter 8

Pacing the Emergency department hallway outside of the examination rooms, Richard rubbed at his temple. He had a headache that just kept growing. He was thankful that they didn't have a team in for training that week but they would have somehow managed that. He turned as he heard footsteps.

Timothy stood beside his boss and friend, worry about Riley uppermost in his mind but also concern for Richard.

"Richard? Have they said anything yet?" Timothy kept his voice low.

"Not yet. Mom and Dad are with Riley right now." Richard was troubled, to say the least, even as he prayed for the lady involved. "Rayleen doesn't have anyone with her. Raleigh is there but she's not family. From what we understand, she has no next of kin."

"See if your parents can go down for now. She needs that. And from what I saw between her and Riley, he would want to be her next of kin." Timothy gave a quick grin as Richard shook his head. "We're praying for all of you. The ladies and Nollan and Sorley are in the chapel. Silas and Madigan are there as well."

"That's what I'm told." Richard looked around as he felt a hand on his shoulder and his father, Reynold, was there. "Dad?"

"I don't want to interrupt you, son, but we would like you to come in with Riley. The doctor wants to speak with us all." Reynold's arm was kept around Richard's shoulders. He had prayed, as had Rose, that Riley would be spared what Richard went through. However, that didn't seem to be the case.

Richard walked away from Timothy, knowing that he didn't need to say anything. They had worked together far too long as a security team, even though they were still young, to have to explain everything.

Timothy watched him walk away, a frown on his face. His head shifted slightly as he heard Naomi beside him.

"How is Riley? Have they said?" Naomi kept her voice low, not wanting to disturb anyone else.

Timothy shook his head. Richard had not said.

"I suspect they haven't been told anything yet. Reynold did just come and get him." Timothy looked around, a sober look to his face. He was worried about Riley, fearing that Riley would be going through what they had all gone through.

"Not likely. Listen, Raleigh is with Rayleen. That lady hasn't roused yet. Do we even know what happened?" Naomi was worried about her friends, knowing just how dangerous it was likely to get.

"I don't know if anything has been said. Jason is with Riley. Lily's with Rayleen?"

Naomi nodded, watching as Lily, a police detective but a good friend, walked rapidly away from the hospital room.

"Lily's leaving. She must have been called out."

"I would think so. Head on back to Rayleen, Naomi. This is where it can get so dangerous, as we know."

"It can. Only God can protect them fully. He uses us but sometimes, we're not enough." Naomi walked away, soberness on her face.

Bill turned from where he had been watching the crime scene techs work away in Rayleen's home. It was strange, he decided, that they were attacked like that. Someone had to be watching them very closely. And that made him fear for his friend and the lady now in his life.

"Sid? What do you have?" Bill waited patiently for the senior tech to compose himself and then speak.

"Who did this, Bill? They were waiting for them. How did they know that they would be home at that time? We checked Riley's truck. There are no trackers on it. We need to see their phones." Sid suspected that a program may have been downloaded to them.

"Riley's can only be accessed by a code. That much I know. I have no idea about Rayleen's. That wasn't something that we discussed." Bill turned away to approach the responding officers. "What can you tell me, fellows?"

Ray, the first officer through the door, shook his head.

"It was strange, Bill. They must have been attacked as soon as they stepped inside. The back door

---

was broken in. That is how they got inside. It looks as if Rayleen was attacked. Riley would have tried to come to her aid and been beaten at that point." Ray was upset. Riley was a good friend and former classmate. "Hasn't Richard's team had enough?"

"They have, but this with Riley? He walked in on something up north a ways. That's why he was with Rayleen." Bill shook his head as he thought back through what he had just witnessed.

Bill had stood off to the side as he had watched the paramedics work on the couple. He could tell by their hurried movements with Riley that he was the more seriously injured of the two. He had helped to shift his friend over to the backboard before helping to lift it and carry Riley out to the stretcher. The paramedics had simply shaken their heads at him as they rushed to assess Riley and then load him into their rig before racing away.

His attention then on Rayleen, Bill had approached her. He frowned. He had no idea why she had been attached. There was not a lot of evidence as to what had happened. The men who had attacked them had been very careful not to move through the house, only to stay in the kitchen area until the couple were in the house. It was frustrating for the investigation, to have them beaten and left to lie for hours that way.

Bill had spoken with Georgia, who was still highly shaken by what she had found. She could give no answers as to who or why. She had not seen anything. In fact, none of the neighbours had seen anything. That was frustrating as well to the investigation.

Walking back through the hospital, Bill found Jason standing outside of Riley's room, his eyes on the family as they spoke with the treating physician. He would not intrude, not until they approached him, but he would need to determine the injuries that Riley had suffered. Lily had been back around, not able to obtain a statement from Rayleen. Until they could do that, their investigation was at a standstill, and no one wanted that.

"Any word?" Bill's voice was low, not loud enough to be heard by anyone other than Jason.

Jason shook his head. He turned as he heard a commotion down the hall before his attention went back to Riley's room.

"None a word. Both of them are still unconscious. Lily did manage to speak with the treatment physician for Rayleen. He didn't say much, she said, other than he needed Rayleen to awaken to properly assess her."

"And they need the same for Riley." Bill walked away again, heading for his office and the work that he was sure was piling up on his desk.

<hr>

Chapter 9

Rayleen began to rouse, not sure where she was. She could hear subtle sounds around her that made her frown. Her eyes opened part way as she looked around. A hospital room? How and why questions surged through her mind.

Sitting abruptly upright, Rayleen waited for her head to stop spinning and the room to steady. She was off the stretcher, heading for the hallway. She was on a search for the man who had tried to protect her.

Standing outside of Riley's room, Rayleen looked around. She didn't see anyone who would stop her from entering but she still hesitated. Walking towards Riley, she frowned. He didn't seem to be awake but he had been beaten. That was obvious.

Her hand rested on his cheek before his head turned and trapped her hand between his face and the pillow. Riley swallowed hard, trying to lubricate his mouth and lips.

"Rayleen? Is that you?" His eyes didn't open as he spoke but she could see the pain on his face.

"It is. Riley? What happened to us?" Rayleen didn't hear the footsteps that paused in the doorway. Rose stood here, coming back to find her son. She had just not expected to find the young lady up and on her feet and with Riley.

"I don't know. I can remember us walking up to your front door and that's it." Riley's eyes finally opened. "Can you remember anything?"

"No, I can't. And we need to. How do we stay safe if we don't know." Rayleen chewed at her lower lip, jumping as she felt an arm around her. Fear shot through her before she heard Riley speak.

"Mom? You're here? Where's Dad?"

"He's with Bill at the moment. They're going through your home, Riley. And this is Rayleen?" Rose hugged the young lady, finding her responding.

"I am. I'm the cause of all this." Rayleen was glum, sure that she would be blamed for it all.

"Not at all. You are not to blame. You are a victim many times over from what I understand." Rose reached to hug her son before her arm was around Rayleen again. "Jason is here to get your statements. I'll be outside. He can tell me when I can come back in."

"Mom? Where's Richard?" Riley thought that his brother would have been there.

"He was here. He's back at his office with his team, starting their investigation. And yes, Emma has reached out to him." Rose walked away, leaving Rayleen staring after her.

"Did your mom really just do that?"

"She did. She had to, Rayleen. We need to speak with Jason." Riley's hand was not letting go of Rayleen even as Jason approached them.

Jason frowned at them, not sure what was going on with his friend, but sure that something was. He looked behind him for a moment as if trying to find some answers that just weren't there.

———

"Riley? What happened this morning?" Jason finally had to ask the questions that were needed.

"I don't know, Jason. I don't remember anything other than walking towards Rayleen's home. We left Richard's early just so that we could go home. Rayleen needed that. What happened at her house?" Riley's question went unanswered for the moment.

"Rayleen? What do you remember?" Jason's voice was firm, bringing her attention to him and away from Riley.

Rayleen shrugged. She didn't remember anything other than being at Richard's home and told Jason that. She could see that he was frustrated, not that she blamed him. But it was what it was.

Jason questioned the couple some more and then walked away, frustrated that he could elicit no further information from them. He paused just outside of the room and turned to study them. He frowned. They looked like a couple but he knew that they were not. At least, that's what he thought.

Riley's gaze followed Jason before he was sitting up on the bed despite Rayleen's protest that he shouldn't be sitting up. He sent his brother's team away, simply stating that they had a life to get to and that for now, he couldn't see what danger that he was in.

Reaching for Rayleen's hand, Riley walked away from the hospital, flanked by his parents. They refused to leave, stating that he needed them and that for the night, the couple would be with them. A friend was repairing the damage done to Rayleen's home.

———

Rayleen had protested at that, stating that she couldn't afford that and that she would do it herself. Riley had simply laughed and hugged her.

"Adam's a good friend. He won't charge you for what he has to do. It's what we do for our friends." Riley nodded at her as he spoke.

"He won't? I don't have friends like that." Rayleen was sober as she spoke. She had felt the lack of friends greatly over the last few years but had been hesitant to reach out.

"We have a great group of friends, darling, and they will just open up to let you in. They have for the spouses." Riley didn't realize what he had implied, but his parents had and shared a look before they nodded. Like Richard, Riley had found his lady and would not be walking away from her.

Rayleen stared up at the tall man who had such a tight grip on her hand and wondered at his words. He didn't mean what he called her, of that she was sure. No man would ever do that. She had locked away the dreams of finding her knight and living the rest of her life with him tight into her heart. Rayleen didn't know that God had heard her unspoken cries for someone of her own and sent Riley into her life.

Rose turned from the kitchen counter, watching Rayleen as she paced the room. She finally just stopped her and hugged her. Rayleen was surprised at that and then hugged Rose back.

"Where are your parents, Rayleen? Can we contact them for you?" Rose frowned at the look on Rayleen's face.

"I have no idea where they are or what they are up to. I lost contact with them a few years ago, by their choice." Rayleen was matter of fact as she spoke. She had come to terms with that years ago.

"They haven't? I am so sorry. But don't worry. We're not walking away from you. Riley won't let us." Rose watched with some amusement as Rayleen scowled at her for a moment.

"What does Riley do anyway for work? No one has ever said." Rayleen jumped as she felt an arm come around her and then leant back against the tall handsome man who seemed determined to protect her.

"What do I do? I'm a paralegal, Rayleen, advocating for low income families. Part of my work is subsided by the Barnabas Foundation, who help out where they are needed, just as encouragers." Riley waited patiently for Rayleen to absorb his words.

"I have heard of them. They work with you?" She looked up at him, not realizing that her heart was in her eyes.

Riley studied her for a moment, seeing the vulnerability that she was showing him. This was not something that he had expected but he shrugged. They had been through too much already to hide how they were feeling.

Chapter 10

Rayleen roamed her home, not feeling safe there any more. She frowned. However that man was who had abducted her? He was still affecting her life and affecting Riley. She had refused to stay at Reynold's and Rose's home, insisting that she needed to be at home. Rayleen had sent a text off to her boss the day before, hearing back from him that he wanted her in the office on Monday, if she was up to coming in. She had been missed greatly. Rayleen had given a small smile at that comment. She wasn't sure that he was correct.

Turning from the back door, Rayleen stared around the kitchen. She was grateful that Riley's friend had stepped in. She just didn't know how much it was going to cost her to have that door and frame replaced. Rayleen didn't believe him that there would be no charge to her. That was not how life worked, as she had found out.

Seeking her rest at last, Rayleen stared at the wall in the darkness. She was afraid, she had to admit to herself. She missed the tall handsome man who'd become a part of her life in the last week, but she was certain that they had gone their separate ways. The chiming of her phone roused her enough to reach for it.

Seeing the message from Riley, Rayleen's face softened. It was just a good night text with a note that he was praying for her. She responded with a thank you and then set her phone to one side. This was not what she had expected at all.

Riley found his prayer corner in the chair in his office that overlooked the back yard. It was a favourite spot of his, one where he had sought his Abba Father and fought out many issues over the years. One of the issues he was struggling with right now was his work. He was no longer satisfied with what he was doing and was praying through a new opportunity that had been presented to him, that of working remotely for the Barnabas Foundation. Riley had not spoken with anyone about it, rather choosing to keep it quiet. He had only asked for prayer for himself with an unspoken request. His family and friends didn't need to know the details but would just pray for him.

A long conversation with Richard had taken place that evening. Richard had tracked him down, not saying anything, but listening to what Riley had to say. The brothers were close and always had been. What Richard had gone through in the previous months had strengthened that bond. Richard had provided what he could with advice and suggestions, knowing full well that they might not work for Riley and Rayleen. He had wanted to ask where Riley's heard was in regards to Rayleen but that wasn't his place. That lady needed to hear from Riley first, if in fact Raleigh was right and Rayleen had Riley's heart.

A sound at his front door had Riley on his feet and cautiously moving that way. He peeked out the door and sighed. Of course, Raleigh's brother, Rori, would show up. They had become close friends.

—

"Rori? What are you doing here?" Riley locked the door behind him.

"Just to pray with you and to watch through the night with you. I know you well, Riley. You're not planning on sleeping until you've prayed this through." He turned and headed for the kitchen, reaching to make a fresh pot of coffee. "We'll need this over night, my friend."

"We will. And thank you, Rori. You are who I need to speak with." Riley was hesitant to speak, not sure how to phrase what he needed to.

"What are you thinking, Riley?" Rori picked up the tray with their coffees and headed for the office, setting the tray down before he found a seat.

"What am I thinking? Right now, I'm not sure what I am to think. Everything is just so confusing."

"Start off with what happened up north. You were drugged, you said."

"I was. I don't remember being locked away but Rayleen said that I was. I fear for that lady, Rori. He'll be after her and soon."

"I heard about what happened to you two. Was it him?" Rori wasn't sure if it had been. He just had to ask to see if Riley had any thoughts.

Riley shrugged, sipping at his mug of coffee.

"I don't know, Rori. I don't remember anything about what happened today and neither does Rayleen. It was too early in the morning for anyone to have been around who might have seen something. We were attacked inside her home. Bill and Jason said that the

___

back door was broken in and that is how our assailants came and went. That doesn't bring a lot of peace of mind to either one of us."

"No, it wouldn't." Rori turned as he heard a tap at the front door. "Were you expecting anyone?"

Riley was shaking his head even as he was on his feet to head that way, Rori trailing after him. He stood with the door open, staring at Rayleen before he wrapped her into a hug and tugged her into the house. He didn't release her even as Rori stepped outside and then walked to Rayleen's house to circle it before he was back inside Riley's.

"Rayleen? What happened?" Riley could feel the shudders that wracked her body.

"I kept hearing taps and sounds outside. I couldn't stay there. I didn't know where else to go. I'm sorry. I'll leave and find somewhere else." Rayleen struggled to escape Riley's hug, just unable to do that. "Riley?"

"Stay here for now, Rayleen. Rori has walked around your house and now called in who we need to." Riley moved Rayleen towards the office, finding a blanket to wrap her in. He turned as Rori appeared briefly in the doorway before he was gone again, this time outside to answer any questions the responding officers might have that he could answer.

Rayleen clutched at the blanket, her fingers white with tension. She shouldn't have come to Riley but she had no idea where to turn. He seemed to be the safest person whom she could run to and she had no idea why she felt that way.

Riley watched Rayleen, not sure why she had shown up at his place but glad that she had. He prayed for his lady, not realizing that was how he thought of her already. He begged God to protect her and to heal her, knowing that she needed that in many ways.

Chapter 11

Lily stood for a moment outside of Rayleen's house, her flashlight shining around as the crime scene techs moved through their processes of collecting information and evidence. She had not been expecting to be called out to a home near Riley's but when she spoke with Bill, he said that would have been expected. She had not heard of the adventure that he had become involved in that included Rayleen.

What she had expected to find was a home that had been broken into again. That was not the case. The techs were finding cameras and motion detection sensors all over the place. She felt it was just too much. Turning as she heard her name called, Lily walked towards Richard, not surprised to see him.

"Richard? You're here?" Lily tucked her pen away into a pocket.

"I am. Riley called me. He has Rayleen with him. She came and found him. I don't know that it was a good thing that she ran from her house in the dark." Richard was frustrated at the situation.

"That's what Rori said. What is the story with them?" Lily was not asking from idle curiosity. Their relationship was a factor in the investigation.

"I don't really know. Bill talked with you?" At Lily's nod, Richard just rubbed at his cheek. "I don't know what is going on. He sent my team home this afternoon. I thought that they were staying with Mom and Dad but Dad called and said that they had headed home.”

“I can see that. Riley is very independent, even more so than you.” Lily turned to study the house in front of her, knowing that they had disturbed the neighbourhood. “Georgia found them this morning, Bill said.”

“She did. I don’t know that there are any easy answers for this, Lily. There never is.” Richard turned and walked away, heading for Riley’s home. He found Rori waiting for him on the city sidewalk in front of Riley’s home. “Rori?”

“They’re inside, Richard. Riley won’t let them leave even though Rayleen has tried to. He’s standing in front of the door, preventing that.” Rori had a grin on his face. “I think that your brother has found his lady.”

Richard shook his head at Rori, even as he grinned at him.

“You think so?” Richard moved past him to head for the front porch, stopping as Rori said something. “What was that you said, Rori?”

“I said that Rayleen is not moving too far from Riley. It’s to be expected, given that he rescued her.” Rori paced towards him, walking up the steps and then tapping at the door before he opened it. He was afraid that Riley had planted himself against the door and that he would hit him by opening it.

Riley stared at Rori and then at Richard, his eyes closing as he saw his brother. He had not expected

———

63

Richard to show up but he should have. Rori would have called him.

"Richard?" Riley's voice brought Richard's head up. "You just had to come."

"Riley, I'm your brother. Of course, I would come. And the team is praying for you and Rayleen. Now, what can you tell me?" Richard closed the door behind him before moving past his brother towards the kitchen. He stopped as he saw Rayleen standing in the middle of that room, a lost and forlorn look on her face before Riley was past him and wrapping Rayleen into a hug. "Rayleen? What happened tonight? What brought you to Riley?"

Rayleen shrugged. She wasn't sure what had actually happened but she only felt safe with Riley. Given that he had rescued her from her kidnapper, it was only natural. But she sensed that there was more to her feelings for Riley than just that. And the look in that man's eyes when he looked at her told her that he was developing feelings for her.

"I don't know, Richard. I really don't know. I just didn't feel safe there. Does that make any sense at all?" Rayleen's hand reached for a chair before she pulled it out and was sitting, her eyes not leaving Richard's face.

"It does, Rayleen. I have a security team. We used to go out and protect people but do the training for that now. What you are saying was common for them to say. Sometimes you feel danger without realizing where it is and how close it is to you. That's where God is protecting you. He's giving you that

—

sense that you need to flee and provides the opportunity for you to do so. We think of God's protection as being visible. Sometimes, it's not. Sometimes it just the sense that we are in danger and we need to react."

Rayleen was nodding. She knew that feeling but had been unable to act on it until Riley showed up.

"There was an angel with me, do you know that?" Rayleen was almost afraid to voice that.

"I know there was. Riley saw him. God sent His angel to protect you until He could send someone to help you. That person was Riley." Richard shared a look with his brother, seeing the turmoil that was going on inside him. "Riley is not walking away from you, not while you are in danger. None of us are. My team will be reaching out to you both to see how we can protect you. The two ladies on my team and the three wives will also reach out to you. And I can guarantee that Lily, a police detective and good friend, will as well as Bill's wife, Jason's wife, and our police chief, Andrew's, wife will as well. They have all had what we term as adventures. We have a large group of friends that God led and protected. They will all be willing to share their stories with you at any time of the day or night."

"They will? I've seen them around church but didn't realize that they had been in danger. Not at all." Rayleen yawned, her head going down on her folded arms as she slept. Riley gave a soft smile before he gathered her into his arms and headed for the living room. Richard was there, reaching for a blanket to

———

65

cover her. Riley tucked it around her, a hand resting on her cheek for a moment as he prayed for her.

"Riley?" Richard spoke softly as he pointed towards the front door. "We need to speak with Lily, if she'll talk with us."

Lily watched as Riley stepped out onto his front porch, assessing him. Bill and Jason were correct, she decided. He was hurting in many ways, not the least of which was the beating that he had taken just that morning. And they were no closer to knowing the reason for that, other than for Rayleen.

"Riley? What have you gone and done?" Lily's comment was spoken lightheartedly even though she knew that he was in danger.

"I have no idea, Lily. I don't know who that man was who kept me captive. I had never been there before." Riley frowned, thinking back on his trip. "I took a wrong turn that day, or rather God had me take a right turn. Who knows how long Rayleen would have been held there."

"That's what I don't understand, Riley. Why kidnap her and take her up there? What did he want from her?" Lily was puzzled by that, needing to make sense of everything and not able to.

"I don't know, Lily. Rayleen doesn't know either. And that is something that we need to determine in order to protect her." Riley walked away to circle his house, leaving Richard and Lily watching him as best that they could in the dark.

Chapter 12

Rousing early the next morning, Rayleen stared around at the living room and frowned. This was not her home. Where was she? On her feet, Rayleen headed for the front door, pausing on the sidewalk before she just walked back to her home. She didn't think to leave a note for Riley or that he would miss her.

Riley walked back through his home, not surprised to see that Rayleen had left. He stepped outside and watched as she headed for her home. He would find her later that day and just take her to church with him. His body was hurting more this morning that he thought that it would but he was determined to be at church. Bruising on his face would give the fact away that he had been beaten, but that was the least of his worries. The main worry was the lady down the street who had just walked away from his home.

Two hours later, Rayleen stared at Riley as he stood in front of her, his hand extended to her.

"We're going to the same place, Rayleen. Let me drive us. That way, you can protect me." He kept grinning at her until she shook her head and took his hand. Tucking Rayleen into his truck, Riley frowned. How had his truck appeared at his home? He didn't drive it there. That meant someone had and he was suddenly afraid because of that. They knew where they lived and could reach out at any time for them.

Standing in his kitchen late that evening, Riley rubbed at his face. He was hurting all over but his heart seemed to be hurting the most. Rayleen was scared of someone and Riley's feeling was that it wasn't her abductor. That man had not appeared even though they had expected him to.

He turned as he heard his phone chime and reached for it. A friend from another town, Abe Finlay, had reached out, just asking what he and his security team could do for Riley and Rayleen. He also commented that his wife, Emma, was starting her search, determined to find the ones responsible. Riley smiled at that. Yes, Emma would find the ones responsible, that much he knew. It was what she did and she was very good at that, finding people that no one else could.

Richard paused in his office doorway, troubled about Riley. They had no answers, no matter how much his team had started to dig into whatever it was. There was just not enough information to move forward. And if they were not able to move forward with the investigation, that left Riley and Rayleen vulnerable to whoever it was that was after them. Richard sighed. They just didn't know why and that frustrated him.

Raleigh approached Richard, reaching to hug her groom as she still called him.

"What can we do, Richard?"

Richard shrugged. There wasn't a lot that they could do.

"I don't know, sweetheart. I really don't. I talked to Dad earlier. He's beyond worried about Riley. We don't know if it's something to do with his work, or if it just coincidental to where he was." Richard stared down at his bride, a frown on his face. "What are you thinking?"

"Why was Riley there? Is it somewhere that he's been before?"

"Not that I know of. He says that he just took off for the week and was driving aimlessly around. He stopped there to grab a coffee which he wishes now that he hadn't."

"But if he hadn't, then Rayleen would still be a captive, and who knows what would have happened to her. Us ladies are meeting tomorrow to pray for them. You don't have a team in tomorrow so you're working on this?"

"We are. Emma and Abe have reached out as has Don. We're going to be working on this together, I would assume, just like everyone else." Richard turned back to stare at the office. "We need to pray for Riley, sweetheart. His adventure is just beginning. I fear for him."

"I know that you do. So do I. Did you know how restless he's been over the last couple of months?"

"No, I didn't. He hasn't said anything." Richard studied Raleigh, knowing full well that she had picked up on something with his brother. "What are you thinking?"

"I'm thinking that he doesn't like his work any more and is wanting to move on. Only, he's not sure what he wants to do. This work has him burning out."

Raleigh's head went down against Richard. "How do we help him, other than praying for him?"

"That's about all we can do, sweetheart. Here. Let's find our prayer corner and pray for the two of them." He looked down at her again as he heard a soft laugh. "Raleigh?"

"Riley is so like you. He's trying had to protect Rayleen and finding it a battle to do so. She's not backing down from him. She's going to be back out there doing what she has to and not thinking of the consequences once she feels safe again."

"That's so true." Richard sighed as his phone chimed and he walked over to his desk. Signing into it, he frowned at the text message. "Rayleen is reaching out. She wants me to keep Riley away from her." He laughed at the snort that Raleigh gave. "No? Don't think that's possible?"

Raleigh shook her head.

"He's like you, love. He will not walk away from her while she's in danger. And that puts him danger as well. How do we solve this before he's hurt worse?"

"That I don't know, sweetheart. Only God knows that and He is their Protector and Avenger. We have to trust in Him."

Riley stood on his back deck early the next morning. He had been unable to sleep, spending the night in prayer and waiting before his Abba Father. He looked up at the sky, seeing the dawn creeping in. It was going to be a hot day in more ways than one, he decided. Riley turned back into his home, not seeing the men hovering around the back of his yard, waiting for him to approach. When he did that, they were prepared to take him and take him away once more. Their plan was to use him to reach Rayleen. Only Riley was not cooperating with them.

Riley turned as he locked the back door, hesitation on his part to be out in the yard that he loved. Someone was out there. He knew full well that even if he called in it, they would be gone by the time the authorities arrived. Riley shrugged, heading for his bedroom and a shower. Dressing in his work clothes, he stared at himself in the mirror. He needed to make a decision soon on where he wanted to be and what he wanted to do. That decision was proving harder than he thought.

Chapter 13

Three days later, Riley once more moved restlessly through his office. He had made a decision to close it, not sure if it was the right one, but he no longer felt that he was in the right line of work. Just what he should be doing? That he wasn't sure of. Riley was praying it through, but also seeking counsel from his father and from his pastor.

Rayleen was watching him closely over the hours that they were together. She needed to be working as well. Only she felt watched and threatened. Her employer no longer allowed her to be out on her own. If she had to be in the field, someone was with her, either one of her fellow employees or a security personnel. Richard's team was picking that up for her as well as Don's team, a close friend of Richard's. She had protested at first, not wanting to put anyone at risk but had lost that argument. Riley had had no sympathy for her when she had complained, merely grinning at her. He knew full well that Richard and Don would be there, even if she couldn't see them. It was what they did.

Turning as he heard footsteps coming towards him, Riley tensed. He had lost his trust in his ability to defend himself since his beating. His heart raced as he moved cautiously to the door and peeked around it. He relaxed as he saw Richard.

"Richard? What are you doing here?" Riley's question didn't surprise his brother.

"Looking for you. We need to talk, Riley, and not about what you are going through. I am looking to add someone to my team and you fit the bill." Richard grinned at his brother. "You know that I have always wanted a paralegal to do training for us. Will you pray about that? I would love to have you work with us."

Riley nodded, knowing that Richard would have prayed this through before he asked him.

"When do you need to know?" Riley wasn't surprised when Richard just shrugged. "Okay. I can do that. I have already made the decision to close my office. Someone else is ready to pick up what I do. I just don't feel it is where God wants me now."

"That's what I'm sensing, Ry. If you come and work with me, I would like that. If not, we'll pray you find the place that you need to be." Richard grew silent for a moment, studying his brother, seeing the lines of stress in his face and the agitation not normally found in his body. "How are you really doing?"

Riley shrugged. He had no idea how to respond to that. He knew that his family and friends were praying for him.

"I worry about Rayleen. She's been put into something that she shouldn't have. And we have no clear picture why. I talked to Emma last night. She called just to see how I was." Riley spoke about a friend of theirs who had a business where she could people and information that no one else could. She just couldn't explain how she did.

"She would reach out. I spoke with Abe as well. He's worried about you, Ry. How do we do this? How do we keep you two safe from someone out there?” Richard gave a partial grin as Riley laughed.

“About as well as you did for yourself.” Riley sighed. “This is not how I planned my week away. I still need that but won’t go anywhere. Not while Rayleen is in danger. And I want to relieve that danger and be with her all the time to protect her. That just isn’t possible.” Riley walked back into his office, stuffing paperwork into his briefcase, and then heading for the door.

Richard followed him, walking around the truck and then back to stand near Riley as he locked up his building.

“It is hard when we want to protect our ladies. It isn’t always possible. How be you and Rayleen come for a meal this weekend? You two need that. And Mom and Dad expect us for a meal as well.” Richard grinned at Riley as he shook his head.

“I can’t force her, Richard. I’ll ask but I don’t expect that she’ll be willing to do that.”

Richard nodded, walking towards his truck with the intent to follow Riley home. Neither man expected to see Rayleen sitting on Riley’s front porch, distress on her face.

Riley was beside her, hugging her.

“What happened, sweetheart?” Riley could feel the tension and fear in her body.

“I have to leave my work, Riley. It’s too dangerous.” Rayleen blinked back tears. “I don’t cry, you know.”

"I know you don't. These are extraordinary circumstances." Riley simply tightened his hold on his lady, watching as Richard searched around the outside of his home and then headed inside. "What can I do for you?"

"What can you do for me? Find out who it is and stop them. We can't live our lives like this." Rayleen glanced up at Riley at that point, her eyes stopping as she saw the look in his eyes, a look that said he cherished and loved her and that he would do his utmost to protect her. "Riley?" Her voice was barely above a whisper.

"We'll talk, sweetheart. We'll talk. For now, let's head inside and speak with Richard. He wants to know why you're here and what scared you so badly that you feel that you need to quit your work." Riley was on his feet, drawing Rayleen into his home, shaking his head at Richard.

Richard sighed. Something had to have happened that day for Rayleen to be acting as she was. And he wanted whoever it was. It had been bad enough that he and Raleigh had been forced to marry and then faced extreme danger. He didn't want his younger brother to face the same.

Riley shot a look at his brother before he stepped back from Rayleen. He studied the beautiful lady standing in front of him. He shook his head.

"I have no idea how to do that, Rayleen. We're trying. Richard's team is trying. Bill, Lily, and Jason are trying. Our friends are trying. They just don't have the right information yet to do just that. And I wish

---

that they did. You're a beautiful lady whom I'd like to date and this is getting in our way." Riley didn't heard his words but Rayleen did.

Rayleen moved into Riley's space, not seeing the look on Richard's face as he left. She reached to hug Riley, surprising him.

"Riley? What you said? Did you mean it?" Rayleen prayed that he had. She had come to the conclusion that he was her knight in shining armour.

"What did I say?" Riley frowned at her for a moment before he thought back over his words. His eyes slid closed. He d\hadn't meant to put that out there, not yet.

"That you wanted to date me?" Rayleen almost held her breath as she waited for him to respond.

"I did. I didn't mean to say it just yet. I'm not sure that you're ready for that." Riley bit at his lip, not sure how to express himself. He found himself the recipient of a hard hug before Rayleen was walking away, leaving him staring after her.

Chapter 14

Looking around as she heard her name called, Rayleen paused. Raleigh was walking towards her with some other ladies. She frowned and then the frown cleared. Two were from Richard's team, Silver and Naomi, and the other two were the wives of the other two members, Tate and Shanli. Riley had warned her, with a grin on his face, that they would be looking for her at some point. Rayleen was surprised with the five ladies hugged her before turning her towards the local diner. Ev, the diner owner, looked up before she was waving the ladies towards her and then pointing towards a private room.

Rayleen's feet stopped, even as Raleigh's arm around her tried to move her forward towards that room.

"We can't go in there. She must have made a mistake." Rayleen looked at the ladies as they all gave a soft laugh.

"No, Ev does that. We'll have privacy there and it will help to keep you safe." Shanli linked an arm with Rayleen. "In case you didn't know it, Ev is aunt to our police chief, Andrew, and I would suspect that Avery, Andrew's cousin, is working today. He's in law enforcement as well."

Rayleen stared at each of the ladies in turn and then shrugged. What was it to her if Ev lost out on business because of this? It was her diner. She looked up briefly at the ceiling, a thank you prayer raised to her Abba Father.

"Okay, then. We're meeting today? Who decided on that?" She grinned as the ladies laughed, hearing other footsteps behind them. She turned to see four other ladies approaching her.

Andrew's wife, Phoebe, Bill's wife, Cora, their pastor, Silas' wife, Madigan, and Lily were all there. This group of ladies were all good friends with one another, drawing from each other as they needed to.

"We have a good group of friends, Rayleen. There are others who you likely know that are friends with us." Cora named them, finding Rayleen nodding.

"I know them from around town and church." She frowned at Cora. "Don't tell me. All of you?"

The ladies laughed as they settled down around a table, knowing that Ev herself would be their server or that Avery would be.

"We all had adventures that you need to hear, Rayleen. You are not alone, never again." Phoebe was adamant about that. "And we have many other friends who will step in and speak with you. Richard has a close friend, Don, who also has a security team. His whole team of six went though adventures as we call them. And we do like to tag along on the adventures. Our perspectives help to a certain degree. We can never totally understand what you are going through, but what we went through? It changed us but has also drawn us closer to one another. We support each other in a way that someone who has not faced life and death struggles cannot."

Laughter filled the room as the ladies relaxed with one another. Rayleen was surprised at how she was accepted into the group, not sure that she should have been. Raleigh had seated herself beside Rayleen, knowing from Richard that Riley was interested in the lady and that the lady seemed interested in Riley. She nodded to herself. Rayleen was just who Riley needed.

"Rayleen? What about your family?" Raleigh kept her voice low enough that no one else would be able to hear her.

"My family?" Rayleen shrugged. "I have no idea where they are at present. We're not close, in case you missed that. They weren't looking for me. I'm not sure if I was ever put down as missing." She blinked, accepting the fact that she might not have. "Unless my employer did." Rayleen sighed. "I can't work any more. I'm too much trouble and danger to have around them. He didn't want me to quit but instead asked that I take a leave of absence." She looked up at that point, finding all the ladies focused on her.

"We all felt like that at some point, Rayleen." Naomi spoke for the group. She shared a look with Silver. "Even though Silver and I are on a security team, we still felt that we were a danger to our team mates. We could and would have quit but Richard simply refused to let us. And Riley is the same. He won't let you walk away from this town, not if he can help it. He's trying to take care of you in his own way."

"He is. I just don't want to put him in any more danger than he is." Rayleen sighed. "And you're telling me that he'd still be there if I did send him away."

—

"He would be." Madigan spoke up at that point. "It's in their character to try and take care of us. All of the men in our lives do that. Listen, I need to run but are we still on for our Bible study and prayer tomorrow night? Rayleen, you must join us. It's our group of friends who meet, just to support one another." Madigan stopped to hug Rayleen before she was away.

Rayleen blinked back tears. She had never been part of a friend group before. She had in fact had a lonely life, not willing to step forward and insert herself into any group.

"Thank you, ladies. I would like that. I have never had that in my life." Rayleen didn't look up, not wanting to see pity on their faces.

Raleigh simply hugged the lady she was convinced would be her sister-in-law. She and Richard had discussed that, Richard simply shrugging. He had no idea what his brother's thoughts were. Riley was hard to read at times and this was one of them.

Walking through her house early that evening, Rayleen felt uncomfortable. She knew that the security system had been upgraded but she still felt as if someone had been inside her home. Hearing a knock at the door, Rayleen jumped before she crept towards the door and peeked out. Richard and Timothy stood there, grim looks on their faces, and she could see Riley rapidly walking up her front walk.

"What are you three doing here?" Rayleen planted herself in the doorway, not willing to admit that she was afraid.

"Someone has been in your home, Rayleen." Richard watched with compassion as she finally nodded. "You know that you did give us permission to monitor your security feed for now."

"I did. I just didn't think it would ever be necessary." She reached for her purse and then for Riley's hand. "I'm thinking that I'll be at Riley's. Here are my keys. Find me when you're done." Rayleen walked away from her home, her hand tight in Riley.

Riley had shared a look with his brother, the sternness on their faces deepening. This should not have happened but it had. Now they had to track through her house to see what had happened. Timothy was sure that something had.

Chapter 15

Bill was angry. This should not have happened, he simply stated to Jason. How did that man get into her home? The locks were some of the best that he had seen. Her security system had been upgraded by Richard's team. Yet, that man made it into her home and planted bugs and a bomb. It had been God, they both decided, Who stopped Rayleen from entering and sent her away.

Richard stood on Riley's sidewalk where he could watch both Rayleen's home and Riley's home. Riley and Rayleen stood on his front porch, their eyes on Richard, waiting for him to react in some way. Richard sighed. This was not how the day was to go. Not one bit. He feared for his brother's life now more than he had.

"Richard? What can you tell us? What are you seeing?" Riley refused to move forward, holding Rayleen back as well. This would be the perfect opportunity for someone to kidnap them once more.

"Not a lot. Bill and his team are still moving around. And I don't like the fact that the bomb squad has just shown up." Richard heard a strangled sound from Rayleen and spun to face her. "Rayleen?"

"Did you say the bomb squad? What did whoever it was do?" She spun and ran into the house, the door closing quietly behind her. Riley knew that his parents were there and that his mother would do her best to comfort and console his lady.

—

Abe and Emma Finlay carefully approached Richard, their gaze shifting between the houses. Richard turned as he heard their footsteps, reaching to hug Emma and then shake Abe's hand.

"You two are here."

"We are. What's going on?" Abe paused beside Richard as Emma approached Riley. The two men could hear a bit of quiet conversation before they heard the house door close again. By then, Riley was standing beside his brother.

"Something is off in Rayleen's home. I would suspect that Bill found a bomb, given that the squad is there." Richard nodded that way. "What have you to say, Abe?"

Abe grinned at his friend and his brother before he sobered.

"Emma has information for you and also for Bill and his team. She's not liking what she found out about that man. But then, she never does, does she?" That brought a quick laugh from the brothers.

"No, I can't say that she ever does. It's that bad that you two are here?" Riley sighed. "I'm going in. Call us when we can go back to Rayleen's." He walked away, knowing that Richard and Abe would not move from where they were standing until they had some answers.

Rayleen turned as she felt an arm around her and just clung to Riley. His arms held her tight as his cheek rested against her head. His eyes were on Emma, who looked distressed, something not common for her.

———

"Emma? What did you find?" Riley's quiet question broke through the silence in the room. His parents stood there, troubled looks on their faces.

"What did I find? That man who held Rayleen captive? He's a second cousin to her. He's been watching her for years at her father's request." Emma paced, thinking through what information that she could share. "I had no idea that he would be distantly related to her."

"It makes sense in the worst kind of way then. He's known where she was and has followed her in order to kidnap her. I just don't understand why." Riley's arms tightened on his lady as he felt the suppressed sobs shaking her body. "Rayleen? We'll figure it out and keep you as safe as we can. That's our promise and commitment to you. Emma has information that she'll want to go over with us. And she'll have passed it on to Bill as well. It's what she does." Riley tried had to step back from Rayleen but found the lady just was refusing to let go of him.

Fear was driving Rayleen not to release Riley even though she knew that she had to. He was her safety line right now. She felt him shifting on his feet and then sitting, wrapping her into tighter into his arms as he pulled her down on to his knee. Her head rested against him as her eyes closed and she prayed. The sounds in the room faded as she slept.

Riley tilted his head to watch her, a soft sound coming from him. He knew that he should be heading for the living room and the couch to lay Rayleen down. That wasn't happening, not right then. They needed Bill to come and tell them what he and his team had found. That wasn't happening either, by the looks of it, not right then.

To say that Bill was frustrated would be an understatement. There was no evidence of how the men were able to access Rayleen's home. The door was not broken in at all. The security feed had gone down for approximately five minutes and that is when Bill and his team assumed that the home was broken into. Nothing seemed out of place but then Bill didn't know Rayleen and had not been in her home prior to this.

He walked away, heading for where he could see Richard. He sighed. This was not how the day was to go. Lily and Jason had been called away to other crime scenes. Like always, when a friend was in danger, the cases seemed to grow.

Richard simply pointed towards the house, turning and walking into his brother's home, hearing Bill's footsteps following him. He shook his head at his parents before he looked for Riley. Richard gave a small smile as he saw Riley simply holding his lady and letting her sleep.

Riley looked up as he heard other people in his home and nodded at Richard. He would need to awaken Rayleen and was very reluctant to do so. He could see the dark circles under her eyes, dark circles that meant she was not sleeping well if at all.

"Bill?" Riley kept his voice low. "What did you find?"

—

"I have no idea, Riley. I need Rayleen awake to go through her home. Can we do that?" Bill found a seat as he stared back at Riley.

Riley was reluctant to awaken his lady but knew that he had to. He softly spoke to her, drawing her attention as she woke to him. Rayleen stared at him, wondering that he was so close to her before she realized that he was holding her. She snuggled down against him, a yawn drawn from her.

"You woke me up, Riley. This had better be good." She could hear soft laughter around her and her eyes slid closed. They were not alone.

"Bill's here. He needs you to go through your home. Can we do that?" Riley watched as she frowned at him and then turned her head to frown at Bill.

"Only if you're there. I won't move without that." Rayleen was on her feet, finding Riley was as well and reaching for her hand. Bill simply shook his head once more.

Chapter 16

Hesitating to enter her home, Rayleen's hand tightened on Riley's. He made no move to force her forward. Instead, he waited for Rayleen to decide if she was going in or not. Rayleen finally sighed and stepped across the threshold, not sure what she would find. She walked through her house, her hand still in Riley's, with Bill and a crime scene tech following her.

Frowning, Riley turned back to Bill. She shook her head.

"I don't see anything missing or anything that doesn't belong here. You've searched, correct?"

Bill nodded. They had made a thorough search and left debris in their wake. He would need to find someone to come in and clean for her. His phone chimed with a text message. As he pulled it out and read it, he smiled. God was at work again. Madigan and Silas were outside. Somehow, they knew that cleaning needed to be done and Madigan had borrowed one of her parents' work vans for the cleaning business that they ran.

"Madigan and Silas are outside, Rayleen. They'll be cleaning your home for you."

Rayleen frowned for a moment before her face cleared. She remembered the cleaning business.

"Okay, so now what, Bill? There is no evidence that I can see of anything missing, changed or added. Did you check the fridge and freezer?" She smirked at him for a moment as he frowned in turn at her and then nodded.

"We did. Anything that is open? It's gone. Cora and Raleigh are doing a food run for you. It's how we are the hands and feet for God on earth." Bill grinned as she shook a finger at him.

Her eyes tracked past Bill for a moment before she was at the light-yellow walls and pulling off a photo.

"This is not mine. Is this what they did?" She handed the photo to the tech who had pulled on latex gloves.

Bill shifted so that he could study the photo. It was simply a landscape picture, which made no sense.

"Do you recognize the area, Rayleen?" He waited for her to speak, living his face to study her.

"I do, unfortunately. It is at a cabin where my parents used to vacation. It is near to that store. Will I never be free of that man?" Rayleen stalked away, fear wafting through her. Who was doing this and why? Those were questions that no one seemed to have an answer for and she desperately needed and wanted one.

Riley watched her walk away before he turned back to Bill. He stepped closer to his friend to study the photo. He sighed. He had been in that area the week before he was taken captive.

"I was there, Bill, the week before, just looking around. I needed a break and that's where I was headed. I had no intention of going there. God must have led me to there and then back there the next week. Rayleen needed me." Riley walked away as well, heading for where Richard was waiting. "Richard? How deep into the investigation are you?"

"Not as deep as we would like to be. Abe and Emma had to leave but they left a raft of material for us. We'll meet tomorrow at the building. We don't have a team in for training."

"I can't. I have meetings all day that I can't reschedule." Riley was frustrated. He searched the area around him, feeling himself being watched but not seeing anyone other than neighbours. He didn't suspect any of them but he was well aware that it was possible that they were part of what was happening.

A week later, Rayleen roamed the downtown area of Elmton. She was back working but only part-time and that only in the office. That frustrated her. She wanted to be out in the field but totally understood why she couldn't be. It would be putting others at risk as she would have to have someone with her.

Madigan and Phoebe watched Rayleen before they shared a look and hurried to catch up with her. They could see Silver and Naomi heading towards them, stopping Rayleen in her tracks.

"How about we do lunch, ladies?" Madigan reached to hug Rayleen, surprising that lady.

"Lunch? Is it that time of day?" Rayleen blinked, a look of shock on her face. "I did not realize that it was that late. Sure. Are you four okay with me being in danger?" She looked at them as they all laughed.

—

"We've been there, Rayleen, all of us. Come on in to Ev's diner and we'll give you the condensed version of what we faced. It was a wild ride. At least only Madigan found a dead body. You remember that, don't you?"

"I do. I was horrified to hear that. I don't know how Madigan could go back into the church again." Rayleen looked at that lady as she laughed.

"It was hard, Rayleen, but I had Silas at my side. We married quickly, you must admit, but we are deeply in love. Having his support over all of that helped as did the prayers from our family, friends, and the church family. It's what has gotten all of us through what we faced. And it will get you and Riley through." Madigan and Silas had talked about that couple, wondering if they were meant to be together. Silas had shrugged and simply stated that it was God's will for that.

"I see. Yes, God does provide." Rayleen stopped speaking, frowning at the couple who had entered and found a seat not far from their table. "Sure, and my parents would show up. What do they want?"

"Your parents? You're not close to them?" Phoebe reached for her phone, sending off a message to Andrew. "I'll let Andrew know and he'll find Bill, Lily, or Jason. One of them will appear and take your parents away for questioning. In the meanwhile, let's enjoy our lunch." She looked up at the man standing beside her. "Avery? You're wearing this hat today."

Avery laughed at her nonsense.

———

"I am for now, Phoebe. What can I get you ladies or do you want what you normally have?" At the chorus of what they normally had, Avery grinned once more and walked away, detouring around the front of the diner just to study the couple. He had overheard Rayleen's words and was worried about her. He knew that she had been on foot that morning, having heard that from the street. He also knew that people on the street were watching out for Riley's lady.

Chapter 17

Riley hesitated as he reached for his office door knob, not willing to open that door. He backed away from it, heading for the back door, only to have something stop him from opening that door. He spun in a circle, not sure which way to turn or where to go. His phone was in his hand as he studied it before he dialled.

"Bill? Where are you?" Riley paced the kitchen area of his building, not wanting to be anywhere but there.

"In your neighbourhood. Why? Where are you?" Bill slowed to make a turn, heading for the downtown area and where he knew that Riley's office was.

"I'm in my office. The thing is I can't get myself to open either door and I don't know why. Right now, I'm pacing the kitchen." Riley turned as he heard a soft sound at the back door. "Someone's trying to get in the back door, Bill. I don't know if you'll be able to make it here in time."

Bill hit the buttons for the siren and lights, calling in for assistance. His car slid to a halt before he was shoving open the driver's door and running for the building. He stared at the doors that were hanging by one hinge, both front and back. Bill drew in a deep breath as he approached the responding office.

"John? What can you tell me?"

John squinted against the bright afternoon light as he pondered Bill's question. He looked around at the spectators, most of them people from the street.

"Riley? He's not there. We can see where he put up a fight. Wasn't he just in danger?"

"He was and he was beaten about 10 days ago. What else can you tell me?" Bill walked quickly towards the building and then through it, seeing the signs of the struggle that Riley put up.

"Not a lot right now, Bill. He tried to get away but he certainly didn't have a chance, did he? They came at him from front and back." John looked around. "We can't tell if he was injured or not. That's part of what we'll be looking for."

"I know." Bill was frustrated and walked away, knowing that he had to call Andrew McBeth, their police chief and a good friend, before he called Riley's family. "Andrew? Riley's disappeared from his building."

Andrew nodded to himself. They were expecting something like this but praying that it didn't happen.

"When?"

"Just in the last ten minutes. I had swung by his home just as he called me stating that he couldn't get out either door. God wouldn't let him." Bill heard Andrew closing his office door. "We'll need to reach out to his family and to Rayleen."

"And Rayleen will blame herself, that much I know. Phoebe's been meeting with her or speaking

—

93

with her. She's not saying what they're talking about but my hunch is just that." Andrew was frustrated as well.

Bill walked away at last from the crime scene, worried about his friend but also worried in how he would approach Riley's family and his lady. He looked up to see Rayleen standing there, arms folded around herself, worry on her face.

"Rayleen? What are you doing here? And just how did you get here?" Bill drew her towards his car.

"I walked here. Riley was to meet me thirty minutes ago and didn't. I came this way looking for him." Rayleen was growing visibly more agitated. "Where is he, Bill?"

"I have no idea at present, Rayleen. Someone has taken him from his office." Bill reached into his car and retrieved a bottle of water which he handed to her. "Here. Drink. You need to after your walk."

Rayleen nodded, rolling the bottle in her hands, not opening it at all. She was puzzled by all this.

"Who did this, Bill? Are you any closer to finding out who took me?" Rayleen didn't think that he was but she had to ask. She could hear the murmur of conversation around her, the sounds of traffic, and the intermittent sounds of nature. The heat rising from the pavement shimmered in waves in front of her eyes.

"I don't know, Rayleen. We're just beginning out work of determining that. You didn't hear or see anything?"

"No, I didn't. I was at work until about three, headed home, and then realized that Riley wasn't there." Rayleen looked up, a lost look on her face. "Where is he, Bill?"

Bill drew in a deep breath. He didn't like the lostness that showed on Rayleen's face or the way her shoulders slumped in despair. Her head was down so that he couldn't see her eyes, but Bill had a good idea of what they would show. He had seen it too many times in the past.

"Rayleen? Here. Sit in my car for now. I'll be a while. Or can I call someone for you?" Bill's hand on her right arm directed her back to his car. Opening the door, he gently shoved her down.

"I don't know who to call. My family doesn't want me and hasn't for years. I can't go to Riley's family. They'll blame me, I just know that." Her words died away as she looked around, anger suddenly on her face. "My father? Why is he here?"

Bill looked around, narrowing his eyes at the man who stood not watching the building but watching Rayleen. His slight gesture to one of the officers nearby had the man heading for Rayleen's father. That man tried to walk or almost run away but was trapped between two officers before he was led away. Bill couldn't hear what he was saying but he could hear the angry voice. He sighed. This is not what was needed at this crime scene, extra drama and a witness threatened. And that was what he took the man's presence to mean, a threat against Rayleen.

Rayleen walked slowly through her home, not really seeing anything. She was afraid, more afraid now that Riley was gone and afraid now that her father had appeared. She heard her phone and tiptoed towards where it laid on the counter. A sad smile crossed her face as she read the text message before she was away to her bedroom, packing a bag and then standing right inside her front door, watching for Richard to appear. He was on his way to pick her up and take her to his parents. That was what Riley would have wanted, he simply stated. Only that never happened.

Chapter 18

Bill had finally walked away from Riley's business address, not happy or content that they had no further information on what had happened to him. It distressed Bill to no end that another friend was facing what Riley was. They had all prayed that no more friends went through anything.

Pausing at his vehicle, Bill stared at it. He needed to track down Rayleen, just to ensure that she was safe. She had sent him a text to let him know that she was at home but only after he had sent her multiple text messages. That was not how life was to be, Bill knew, but it was what it was.

Rayleen watched from what she thought was the safety of her house as Bill walked towards her. She sighed. She sensed that he was not happy with her, but her decision to walk away from him at the crime scene had been just that, her decision.

Bill looked up at the sky. It was starting to head towards evening. They were no further ahead knowing where Riley was. He had reached out to his family who were very much concerned about him. Richard hadn't said anything but then again, he didn't. He knew only too well what had happened and what Riley was facing. He didn't want that for his brother but it had happened. His teams and his friends were searching for his brother. His other concern had been Rayleen. Was she safe?

"Rayleen? Do you know how much danger you were in to walk away like that?" Bill's words bit at her.

Rayleen glared at him before she shook her head. Of course, she knew. She had felt someone walking behind her, someone who would make an attempt on her life. Rayleen was convinced that she would be killed and that there was nothing anyone could do to prevent it.

"I know, Bill." Rayleen stood her ground, not backing away from Bill as he stood in front of her. Her head turned as she heard an odd sound from inside her house and then spun to enter it.

Bill almost jumped for Rayleen as he caught at her arm and pulled her away from the house. Rayleen fought him the whole time, the whole time, that is, until the explosion sent the two flying through the air to land heavily on the ground and then not move.

Debris floated through the air, to land heavily on them and then around them. The house shuddered on what was holding it upright, which was not much. Neighbours ran from their homes and then towards the couple, their phones out to make the call to the emergency services. It was not long before sirens sounded and then the red and blue lights of the emergency services flickered through the air.

Andrew ran towards the couple, Lily and Jason keeping pace with him. He was horrified to find that it was Bill that had been hurt yet again helping out a friend. He stood, his eyes on Bill and then Rayleen before he looked towards the house.

"Find out what happened, Lily. Jason? You know what you need to do. We're not getting in there, not by the looks of it." Andrew was frustrated that they could not access the building.

"No, I don't think that we will be. I'll do what I can here. Lily will be going with them?" Jason had to ask, even though he knew that would be the case.

"She will be. I'm heading back to the office. I have a meeting that I need to be at." Andrew took one last look at his friend and then walked back to his car. This is not how the day was to end but it had. God was in control and watching out for them, of that Andrew was convinced.

A sudden shout sounded through the air just as Bill and Rayleen's ambulances disappeared. The men and women gathered near the house ran as fast as they could as the house shuddered and then collapsed on itself. They stood in shock, sharing glances with one another before the investigators stalked towards it and around it. This had complicated their work but in other ways, made it easier. They could now have the debris removed safely to allow for an investigation inside to determine what had caused the explosion.

Jason stood watching as the physician assessed Bill. He knew that Cora, Bill's wife, was outside in the waiting room. One of the officers had found her. Their two children had been delivered to Cora's parents, who had been horrified to hear of what had happened.

Lily stood near Rayleen's stretcher, a frown on her face. She knew Rayleen but not her family. They needed to be there but something kept her from reaching out. Lily knew that her father had been arrested earlier that day at the scene near Riley's building. He just wasn't speaking, not at all. And they needed him to.

There was also the concern for Riley uppermost in everyone's mind. Raleigh had appeared at the hospital, asking to be put down as Rayleen's next of kin for now. She needed someone and Raleigh felt strongly about that. She also knew that the other wives were around, Richard's team splitting themselves into two groups, one at Riley's building and the other at Rayleen's home. Richard would float between them and the hospital.

Richard found his seat in the waiting room, his eyes roaming as he searched the room. He should not be here, he knew, but should be out searching for his brothers. That wasn't happening just yet. His brother's lady needed someone with her. He had been shocked when Jason stated that they had arrested her father near Riley's work but that man was not speaking with them. He had even refused a lawyer. Richard shook his head at that. It couldn't be happening yet again, he thought, but God was in control. He knew exactly what He was doing and would be there for Riley and Rayleen, just as He had been for Richard and Raleigh. His hand reached for Raleigh's as she found a seat beside him.

"What are they saying, love?" Richard waited patiently for his wife to speak.

"Not a lot. She's still unconscious. How is Bill?" Raleigh nodded as Richard simply shook his head. They both watched as Cora almost ran for the ward and her husband.

"Dad's coming around, he said. Mom will be here shortly." Raleigh rested her head against her husband. "Do we know why?"

"No, we don't. And with the house collapsing as it did? It's going to take days for them to go through it." Richard was frustrated, yes, and very worried but he knew Who was in control and could only wait on Him. He felt a hand on his shoulder and was on his feet, gathering into his father's hug.

Reynold hugged his oldest son, holding on longer than he usually would. He stepped backwards, his hands on his son's shoulders, wondering at the height of the man standing in front of him, a height that was matched by his brother. Only that brother wasn't there and they had no idea just where he was.

Chapter 19

Rayleen finally began to rouse, not because she wanted to but because someone else seemed determined that she do so. She felt a hand on her arm, resting gently to be sure, but still seeming insistent that she open her eyes. She just didn't want to. She liked the darkness that she was in. Rayleen felt safe to some degree in the darkness, not sure why she would.

Raleigh studied the lady who was important to Riley, wishing that things were different and that Riley had found his lady without going through danger. They still had no idea where he was other than he wasn't where he was supposed to and that was with them. Raleigh's head turned slightly as she heard footsteps approaching her.

Jason stood for a moment, studying his friend, and then turning his attention to Rayleen. His head tilted slightly as he did so, a small smile on his face. She was awake, he decided, just not ready to open her eyes and face them. But face him what exactly what she had to do. An officer had been hurt coming to her aid. Bill was on his feet, shaky as he was and hurting but wanting to be out there on the search for their assailants and also on the search for Riley.

"Rayleen? You do need to wake up. We need to talk." Jason's portfolio hit the bedside table. He shook his head as Raleigh walked away. It was needed, he knew. There was a police officer at her door for now.

Rayleen sighed. God, are You there, her heart whispered. I can't do this any more. Her eyes opened as she looked around, frowning at the hospital room.

"What happened? Jason? Why am I here?" Rayleen could feel panic starting to set in before Jason's head was bowed and he was praying for her.

"What happened? Bill had come to speak with you about why you walked away from Riley's business this morning. He heard a sound and then ran with you from your home. A bomb or something exploded and sent you two flying through the air. Just as you were being taken away from the scene, your home collapsed on itself. It was too badly damaged to stay upright." Jason watched with compassion as her face crumpled and she was unable to control the tears that filled her eyes and trickled down her cheeks.

"That happened? I don't remember. In fact, I don't remember what happened today at all." She looked past him. "Is Riley out there?" When he didn't answer, her gaze went back to him and she frowned at him. "Jason? Where's Riley?"

"Do you know that we arrested your father this morning?" Jason's voice was stern to control his emotions.

"No, I didn't. I just said that I don't remember what happened today." Rayleen's head went back on the pillow. "Why?"

"Why? Why what? Why did we arrest your father?" At her nod, Jason sighed. It would be the luck of the draw for him to have to tell her. He looked around the room, taking in the equipment and supplies that filled the shelves and stood around the room. His attention went back to her. "He was on the scene of a crime and had no good reason for being there. We're finding out some interesting information on him, including that he has been monitoring you all this years since you walked away from them."

"I knew that he likely would be. He wouldn't let me go that easily." Rayleen's eyes closed for a moment as she prayed for strength to go on. "But you haven't said where Riley is."

"We don't know. I'm sorry, Rayleen. Riley disappeared from his building this morning. He called Bill, asking for help. Before anyone arrived, someone broke in and disappeared with him." Jason was frustrated that had happened. "We don't have a lot of information. Bill said that you were there, he spoke with you and had you in his car, and then you disappeared. He had gone to your home to speak with you when that incident occurred."

Rayleen kept her eyes steady on Jason even as she shook with fear. Someone was indeed after her. She didn't know for sure if it was her father or if it was the man from the store.

"Did you ever figure out why I was taken to that store in the first place?" She sighed as Jason shook his head. "I just don't understand any of it. And until we do, nothing will be resolved." She swung her feet of the side of the bed, waiting for her head to clear. "I have to find a place to stay."

"And you have many offers for that. Richard and Raleigh would like you to stay with them. He has a really good security system and his team is in and out over the next days with their training schedule. Their parents have offered as well. You have multiple places to pick from, Rayleen, from our friends. We understand how hard it can be to be where you are. You. need to hear our stories. We promise to do our best to keep you alive." Jason's head turned as Raleigh reappeared. "Here's Raleigh. Talk it over with her where you want to be and then let me know." Jason walked away, hugging Raleigh on the way by.

Raleigh approached Rayleen to sit on the side of the stretcher beside her, not saying anything. There wasn't anything that she could say that would change the situation or help alleviate Rayleen's pain and worry.

"You would let me stay with you?" Rayleen finally spoke, her voice soft but broken.

"We would, Rayleen. Riley would like that. But the choice is yours. We will back you until and unless you are in more danger. Then the team will move in."

"That's what I'm afraid of. The team. And I understand there are two other teams." Rayleen smiled briefly as Raleigh began to laugh, watching as Richard approached them. "Richard?" Rayleen stared at him for a moment before she sighed and slipped down from the bed. She was out of the room and running from the hospital before anyone could stop her.

Richard was on her heels, not finding her. Stephen from his team approached him. Paul from Don's team was beside him. They could see the frustration on Richard's face.

"Richard?" Stephen stared at his boss and friend and then around them. "What happened?"

"Rayleen ran. I have no idea where to start to look to find her. And we need to find her. Her home was a deliberate act, that much we know. How do we keep her safe and protect her if we don't know where she is?" Richard's hands ran through his black hair. This is not how this was to have gone.

Paul gave a quick grin before he sobered.

"We all wanted to do that at some point, Richard. We'll find her. I just don't know how, as you say." He walked away, heading for Don who was watching him. "Don? Rayleen ran."

Don nodded. He watched Richard for a moment, worried about his lifelong friend and his friend's brother.

"We all thought that she would. If she hits the streets, they'll watch out for her. But we don't know if she'll do that. Richard or Jason will reach out to her employer. She'll likely keep working."

Paul was shaking his head. He had spoken with that man only to find out that Rayleen had requested a leave of absence for three weeks. He had no idea what she was facing but he had agreed. Her employer was deeply worried about Rayleen.

Chapter 20

Rayleen stared back at the hospital, not certain that she should have run but she had felt trapped by Raleigh and Richard. She was well aware that they meant her no harm but she was still afraid. And being afraid had driven her to slip away from them. Rayleen turned back to the street, heading away from the large building behind her and towards the downtown area. She no longer had a home and was afraid that her family would once more come into her life. She didn't believe Jason when he said that her father had been arrested. That wouldn't have happened, Rayleen decided.

Walking towards the area away from her home, Rayleen didn't heard the footsteps that approached her and then walked beside her. She felt safe for the moment, not sure why. Her body was in pain and she could feel herself shutting down. Not feeling the hand that encircled her arm, Rayleen just moved with the man who kept constant watch around her.

Old Jim shook his head. This was when Rayleen could easily disappear and never be seen again. He had heard what had happened to her and Riley and had been watching out for Riley's lady. He had been on the scene of the destruction of her home and then headed for where he knew that she was. Old Jim had not expected Rayleen to appear as she had but he moved in to protect her.

Shoving her down gently on the pallet of blankets that he had arranged for his own comfort, Old

Jim stood back. He needed a lady here to look after here. He snapped his fingers before he pulled out the secreted phone from a deep pocket and sent a simple text message. Silver would appear, he knew, knowing that he only asked for help if he really needed it. They were old friends and school mates and helped each other as they were able to.

Silver pulled out her phone, the constant vibration of a text message disturbing her. She shielded the phone from the bright light and then drew in a deep breath. She looked around for Naomi and Timothy, heading towards them.

"Old Jim has found Rayleen." Silver kept her voice low. "He has her safe for now but wants to know where Richard wants her."

"He has? We'll need to head that way. Only we need Stephen." Timothy looked around, not seeing Stephen near them.

"Thomas is free. He'll go." Naomi was away from her friends, reaching out to catch Thomas by the arm. "Thomas? We need you."

Thomas shared a looked with Don who nodded even as he frowned at Naomi.

"Naomi?" Thomas kept his voice low, not sure if anyone was close who could hear them.

"We have word that someone has Rayleen safe. We need to find her. But we need a paramedic with us. Stephen's not available." Naomi's steps stopped by her friends. "Silver?"

"Old Jim has her, as I said. He wants us to wait for night. For now, Rayleen is okay and safe." Silver was frustrated by the whole situation, wishing that it was different but knowing that Rayleen had done what they would have done and that was to run.

In the early morning hours and amid the blackness of the night, such as it was, three dark forms darted quickly through the downtown area, keeping to the shadows as much as they could. They had a destination in mind and were determined to find it. A fourth dark form appeared briefly in a doorway and then disappeared. The three forms chased after him and disappeared as well.

Old Jim turned as he heard the quiet footsteps behind him. He nodded. Silver, Naomi and Thomas had appeared. He had expected Stephen but Thomas was a paramedic and that was what was needed.

"This way, Thomas. She hasn't roused since she laid down." Old Jm led the way and then pointed through an open doorway. He then turned to the two ladies. "You weren't followed."

"Not that we could see but we could have been. We need to move and move quickly." Silver stepped back to the doorway, listening for anyone out there. "Old Jim? Whee is everyone?"

He shrugged, knowing that his friends on the streets were watching out for him and the lady whom they knew was Riley's. They were hidden but were prepared to stop in at any time.

Rayleen roused as she felt an arm under her back. She fought the man trying to raise her into his arms. A lucky or unlucky blow, depending on how you looked at it, hit Thomas in the face, causing him to draw back. Rayleen scrambled on her feet and away from him, terrified that whoever was after her had found her.

Thomas reached for Rayleen's arm again, finding her slipping away from him and running for the door. None of the other three could reach her to stop her in time from racing through it and then into the outdoors. She was gone from sight by the time that they had rushed outside. They searched for Rayleen, to no avail. She had disappeared. All they could do was pray that she was still free and would heal. Naomi reached out to both Richard and Jason, letting them know that Rayleen had once more disappeared from their care.

Richard stared at his text message before he turned to stare out of his kitchen window. Raleigh had retired, hugging him before whispering a prayer for them all. She was afraid for Riley and also Rayleen. No one knew exactly why they had been targeted although she had a good idea that Riley had been taken to have his paralegal skills used. That just left Rayleen's abduction to be explained. And that explanation was no closer to fruition than it had been.

Bill was on his feet and home. Cora and their young children were away with her parents, for which he was grateful. He turned as he heard footsteps and his brother, Wesley, appeared.

"Bill? Should you be up? You just got home." Wesley was worried about his brother, hurt once more in the line of duty. He didn't know how many times that would happen before Bill just gave up being a police officer.

Bill shook his head. He shouldn't have come home. Even the hot shower had not eased the pain of the bruising and soft tissue injuries that he had sustained. And the headache was just not letting up.

"No, I not likely should have. I need to find Rayleen." He staggered as he turned, Wesley's hand on his arm out to steady him. "I hate this, Wesley. How do we ever find either one of them?"

"That is where God comes in. He has them in the hollow of His hand and is protecting them. We'll find them."

"But when we find them, will they still be alive? That's a question I don't want to have the wrong answer to." Bill reached for his mug of coffee, knowing that he had expressed a thought that he rarely shared with someone outside of his force. But then, Wesley was his brother and also a police officer. He knew how Bill would feel.

Chapter 21

Trudging into her office, Rayleen was discouraged, downhearted, exhausted, and worried and hurt beyond what she had ever been. She unlocked her office door and dropped into her desk chair. Her arms folded on her desk top and held her head that suddenly seemed too heavy for her to hold up. She had met with her insurance investigator. What Rayleen had suspected was true. Her home had been an arson fire. Just who or why was undetermined at this point. The investigator had gone over all the details of what she needed to do but he had to admit to himself that he was worried about her. She just wasn't herself and he could understand to a certain extent why. Rayleen had been through the wringer and back as his mother would have said, referring to a wringer washer, something that was no longer in use.

Her employer, John, hesitated in the hallway outside of her office where he could watch her. He hurt for his friend and employee. This should not have happened. He was glad that she was back with the team but he still feared for her. John detoured to the break room and grabbed a bottle of juice for Rayleen and a bottle of water for himself. He was surprised that Rayleen didn't raise her head as he set the juice bottle on her desk and then found a seat in front of that desk. He waited, somewhat impatiently, for Rayleen to respond, praying for her as he did so.

Rayleen stirred, her prayers feeling as if they hadn't even reached the ceiling of her office. Her head raised as she stared at the juice bottle, something that she didn't remember bringing in with her, and then raised further as she heard a voice. That voice caused her to jump in fear.

"John? Where did you come from?" Rayleen's voice was barely a whisper, all the emotions and hurt that she was feeling in it.

"From home." He grinned at her as she attempted a smile at his joke. "Seriously, Rayleen, I put that juice by you and then sat. You didn't move at all until now."

"I know, John. I didn't have anywhere to sleep last night other than in an abandoned building. Someone tried to help me but I can't remember who." Rayleen drew in a deep breath. "My home and everything in it is gone. I need to start over. And right now, I don't have the mental or physical or emotional stamina to do just that." Her hand went up as John's mouth opened. "I know, John. God is with me. He is in control. I know all the platitudes and sayings that everyone utters at times like this. It doesn't make it any easier to bear or understand." Her head dropped back on her arms. "And just where is Riley? Does anyone know."

John prayed audibly for Rayleen, knowing that he didn't have the answers for her.

"What are you doing about somewhere to live?"

Rayleen shrugged. That question was a huge one in her mind. She had stood at the yellow caution tape surrounding what remained of her home. She was thankful that Bill had been there and pulled her from the house, even thought both of them had been injured.

"I don't know, John. I have to find somewhere furnished for now. It will be weeks I'm told before the remnants of my home are released to the insurance company." Rayleen looked up as John made a sound. "John?"

"We have that cottage on the lot next to us, Rayleen. It's yours for the duration at no rent." John's hand went up. "You know that we do that, let people stay for free. This time? It's you that is in need. It's furnished, so you don't have to worry about that. Now, for your personal effects?"

Rayleen nodded, feeling somewhat relieved to have a place to stay. It was the shopping that she dreaded.

"I have to shop, and you know how much I dread that."

"It's okay, Rayleen. Marie was around early this morning and took Evie with her. They're shopping for you. They know you well enough to know what you like. As for the expense, Breck from the Barnabas Foundation reached out. They had heard about your adventure and wanted to help. Everything you need or want or wish for will be provided at no cost. Your car?"

"It was destroyed as well. Not by the fire. Someone was around last night and did that. I was able to retrieve my laptop which holds my life." Rayleen sat back, her eyes on John. "God is doing this, isn't He?"

"Doing what, Rayleen?" John had a good idea of what she meant.

"Providing for me. Looking out for me."

"He does that." John was nodding as he spoke. "And He is protecting you and Riley as well. We both know that."

"We do. I just wish it had been different. I still don't understand why I was abducted all those weeks ago. I was never told and could never find a way to escape, until Riley showed up." Rayleen was on her feet as she heard voices in the hallway. That scared her for a moment until Jason and Lily appeared in her doorway. "I have nothing to say, guys. For now, I have work to do, so you can leave." Rayleen brushed by them, heading for the back of the building and the library of material and information that was contained in one of the rooms.

Jason stared after her, somewhat angry that she had walked away. A touch on his arm from Lily had him looking down at her.

"She's not ready to speak yet, Jason. She may never be. Let me see what I can do." Lily walked after Rayleen, knowing that Rayleen was not likely to open up to her either. She could not find that lady, deducing that Rayleen had simply left the building.

Jason appeared behind Lily, his head stretching forward to look around her. He gave a slight smile.

"She's run?"

"I would suspect that she has for now and is waiting somewhere she can watch us leave. I have her phone number. I'll catch up with her later. I'm worried about her, Jason." Lily turned to her fellow detective. "How do we solve this and soon?"

"That the elephant in the room, Lily. We can't because we don't know who or why. It's like what you and Loch went through as well as all of our other friends. We have to have more information. And I know that Emma and her team are sending us what she has verified. I suspect that she is sending more information to Richard that she has but hasn't got to the point to release to us."

"I would say so. I talked to Naomi earlier. They don't have a team in for training and are trying to solve this and find Riley at the same time. He needs to come home." Lily walked away, leaving Jason staring at the back door of the building before he shook his head and walked back to his car. He needed to be elsewhere as much as he wanted to remain there and wait for Rayleen to reappear.

John stood in the parking lot, watching the detectives leave. He was not surprised to find Rayleen at his shoulder.

"They're gone but they'll be back, won't they?" Rayleen was exhausted, not knowing how she would ever work that day.

"Evie and Marie are on their way here. They're picking you up and taking you to the cottage. I understand that they are going to make sure that you're safe and that you sleep." John grinned at her before he hugged her. "Go on, Rayleen. It's what the team wants for you. They want you back, safe and sound and healthy. We're not leaving you out of anything but for now? Your job and focus has to be on healing."

Rayleen nodded, knowing that John was correct. Each of the team had reached out to her and expressed those very sentiments. She loved her team and knew that what they wanted was for the best of that team.

Chapter 22

Walking through the cottage that afternoon, Rayleen was restless but also terrified. She had felt the men watching her and following her even though she was with others. She was afraid that they would be harmed because of her. And why that was? Not one person could tell Rayleen. She had been grateful for the clothes and other items as well as the food that the ladies had provided for her, albeit bought by the Barnabas Foundation. She had a lot of people to thank, she decided, not sure who to thank first.

A knock at the front door had her spinning, a hand to her mouth to squelch her scream. She snuck towards the door, on her tiptoes to peek outside. Of course it would be Richard and whoever it was that he had with him.

"What do you want?" Rayleen swung the door open, not ready to admit that she welcomed company even if it was Richard.

"We need to talk, Rayleen. In the house." Richard moved her back inside, Stephen beside her. "We need to have Stephen assess you if you won't go in to see a physician. He's the paramedic on my team."

Rayleen reluctantly submitted to Stephen's assessment, her eyes not leaving Richard's face. He stared back at her, his face impassive. It was not the first time that he had been stared at like that and would by far not be the last.

"Rayleen? You shouldn't have left the hospital, you know." Stephen packed away his gear, not moving from where he had sat beside her. His eyes were on her face, seeing the struggles that she was undergoing. He could understand to some extent, having gone through an adventure of his own.

"I know. I just couldn't stay. I felt caged again." Rayleen's eyes clouded for a moment with tears. "Do you know how that feels?"

"We can understand to some extent. And you're right to feel that way. You'll stay alert if you do." Richard watched her closely, seeing just how close to the edge that she was. "And I do know that Riley would want you to take as much care as you can." His hand went up as her mouth opened to protest. "He cares for you, Rayleen. That has been obvious to all of us over the past few days. It doesn't matter if he is here or not. He would be looking after you, and part of how he would do that is to call in my team, our friends with teams, and his friends here, including Bill, Andrew, Jason, and Lily. It's what he does."

"I know that, Richard. He told me that. I just can't do it." She walked away from the two men, to stand with the front door open. "I think that you need to leave."

Rayleen watched as the two men reluctantly took their leave. It was not what they wanted, she could tell, but it was what she wanted and needed. She needed to sleep and that was a priority for her right now. Setting the alarm system, Rayleen headed for the bedroom, dropping down on the bed without even reaching for clean clothes or for a shower. She was that worn out

<hr>

and tired. She didn't hear anything overnight, which surprised her when she was awoken by a beam of sunlight hitting her in the face.

On her feet and showered and in clean clothes, Rayleen headed for the kitchen, intent on finding coffee and then food. Her focus shifted as she heard a tap at the back door. She frowned as she headed for it, not sure what to think or do. Shock covered her face as she stared at the man once she had found enough courage to open the door.

"Riley? How? Where did you come from?" Rayleen's hand reached for his arm, almost tugging him inside violently.

Riley staggered for a moment before he wrapped Rayleen in his arms. He could not explain how he was brought to that place in the middle of the night. He had been too groggy and out of it to really understand what was being said to him. All he knew what that the lady he loved was in that home but that he had to wait for morning to knock at the door. That had taken some convincing for him to agree. Riley had been on his feet as soon as he saw movement through the window. He had not slept, his attention glued to that window, just waiting for Rayleen to appear.

"I don't know, sweetheart. I really don't know. Someone brought me here during the night and made me agree to wait until you were up. Do you know how hard that was?" Riley's arms tightened even more around Rayleen as she hugged him back.

"I see. Here, have a seat. We need to call someone." Rayleen moved to turn away from Riley only to find herself trapped once more in his arms. "Riley?"

"Don't leave me, Rayleen. That's what they told me you had done. That you had packed up and left town. I didn't think that you would." Riley was almost in tears, overwrought and overtired.

"No, I didn't leave town. My house? That's another story. Someone burnt it down on me."

"Your house? That's what they meant then. They told me that you were homeless and that would make it easier to catch you. Only they couldn't find you and blamed me." Riley's eyes closed for a moment, fatigue causing him to sway on the chair.

"You need someone to help you, Riley." Rayleen shoved away from him, searching for her phone, heading instead for the front door. She opened to see Richard standing there with a bag in his hands, Stephen beside him. "Good. You're here. He's in the kitchen and not really coherent." She was away from the two men before they had a chance to respond.

Sharing a look with Stephen, Richard rapidly walked after Rayleen, hearing Stephen shut and lock the door before his footsteps sounded behind him. He froze in the entry way to the kitchen, blinking and then rubbing at his eyes. Riley really was seated there, his head hanging down. He looked rough and hard done by, Richard decided, before he was crouched beside his brother, an arm around him.

"Riley? Where did you come from?" Richard had to ask his question more than once before Riley's head rose.

———

"Where did I come from? I have no idea. And just who are you?" Riley looked past Richard to see Stephen studying him, a puzzled look on his face. "Do I know you?"

Richard sighed. This was just like some of the others, he decided.

"I'm your older brother, Richard. And this is Stephen, the paramedic on my security team. You know us. For now, let Stephen have a look at you before we decide who to call and just where you should be." Richard was on his feet, his hand out to help Riley to his own feet before Stephen's hand was there to assist Riley to walk away. The two men could tell that he was reluctant to leave the lady standing and staring after him.

Chapter 23

Richard paced the kitchen, moving around Rayleen as she just stood and stared towards the hallway. He finally reached to give her a hug before shoving her down on a chair. He sat beside her, not saying anything, just waiting.

"Richard? Is Riley here? I can't believe it!" Her voice was barely above a whisper.

"He is. He found you, somehow, Rayleen. Did he say anything?" Richard watched as her eyes finally turned towards him.

"Just that he was made to sit down outside and had to agree that he wouldn't knock at the door until I was up." Rayleen drew in a shaky breath. "What if I hadn't been here? How long would he have waited?"

Richard nodded. She had asked the questions that he would.

"For a while. I suspect that whoever brought him here was out there watching over him." Richard dropped his head for a moment, relief spreading through him. His phone was out as he sent out text messages to Raleigh, his parents, and then his team members. He looked up at Rayleen. "Did you call anyone?"

Rayleen shook her head. There had been no chance to do that before Richard and Stephen had appeared and she flatly told him that. He grinned at her as she frowned before giving a small tentative smile.

"That's okay, Rayleen. I understand. Now, who do you want me to call?"

Rayleen shrugged. She had no idea who he should call. She really didn't and told him that.

"How be I call Bill and Lily? That will work?" Richard waited patiently for Rayleen to respond, his fingers hovering over the contact list on his phone.

"I guess. Lily was to come around last night. I don't know if she did. I went to sleep as soon as the ladies left." Rayleen groaned. "And I don't know that I thanked them."

"You would have." Richard was on his feet and headed for the front door. Bill and Lily stood on the doorstep, frowning at him.

"What are you doing here, Richard? We're here to see Rayleen." Bill paused, narrowing his eyes as he watched his friend. "When?"

"Sometime overnight. Riley was brought here and had to agree not to knock at the door until Rayleen was up. Knowing Riley, his gaze would not have left the kitchen window until he saw her." Richard sighed. "I haven't asked him anything yet. Stephen's with me and assessed him. It's up to you if you need to have someone else do that, but I don't know that he'll agree, unless Rayleen can talk him into that."

Lily shook her finger at Richard before she was past him and heading for Rayleen. She simply hugged her friend, feeling the sobs shaking her body. "We'll figure it out, Rayleen. We always do."

———

"But will we still be alive?" Rayleen shoved away from Lily and headed for the back patio. She needed to be alone at that moment, just to take in the fact that Riley was home and at her house. She didn't want that. Rayleen wanted Riley to stay away from her, just to stay safe. He needed to be with his family, not realizing that he had claimed her as his family and would be no other place than with her.

Stephen stepped outside, just watching her. He had assessed Riley and knew that he would have to be seen by someone else, just so nothing could be said of the investigation. Riley had not liked that but had nodded as Stephen told him that.

Riley sighed as he watched the door close behind Stephen. Stephen was correct. He would need to be seen by someone else and that he didn't want to do. He wanted to be where Rayleen was. Reaching for the bag of clean clothes, he turned to the shower, the hot water hitting hard on the bruising that he had. He winced, not liking the feeling, but knowing that he would heal at some point.

Walking back through the cottage, Riley's steps paused as he heard both Bill and Lily. He had no idea how they ended up there but he had no choice now but too speak with them. That was not what he wanted. He walked forward enough that he caught Bill's attention.

Bill excused himself and walked toward Riley, finding Riley backing away from him.

"Riley? How did you get here?" Bill kept his voice low, just loud enough for Riley to hear him.

―――

"I don't know. I was in a locked room and then I'm here. Someone brought me here. I have no idea who." Riley rubbed at his face, fatigue almost too much for him to handle. "I need to sit, Bill." He did just that in the first chair that he found, thudding down harder than he planned. He winced at the pain. "You want my statement."

"I do but first, here's some water and a mug of coffee. Do you want any toast?"

Riley nodded. He desperately needed something to eat, not having had a lot over the last few days. He nodded his thanks as Lily handed over a plate and then disappeared to find Rayleen.

"Let me pray wth you first, Riley. That's what you need." Bill bowed his head to pray for his friend. When he looked up, he sighed. He would not be getting any information from Riley at that point. His friend was asleep. Bill rose and found a blanket to cover him before he sought out Lily, simply asking that she stay with Riley and Rayleen until she could get a statement from the man.

Lily nodded. She was due to be off that day but had felt compelled to find Bill. They had headed for Rayleen's home, just to see how she was, not expecting to find Riley there.

"I will. Rayleen needs me here. Stephen is staying and Silver will be around. The others are teaching today, Richard says."

"That's good. Make sure no one else comes around, other than his parents. He needs them." Bill walked away from the cottage, searching the area

around it. He didn't feel watched at that point but he
was sure that whoever it was knew where Rayleen was
and now knew were Riley was.

127

Riley roused a couple of hours later, rubbing at his face and then his eyes. He looked around, a frown on his face. He didn't recognize this place, he decided, and needed to find his own home. He walked away from the cottage, searching for anything that would tell him where he was. Riley was surprised to find himself in his own neighbourhood and quickly made his way to his home, not realizing the fear and consternation that his action created.

Stephen shook his head as he stopped Rayleen in her tracks. He shook his head at her before looking at Lily, who was nodding at him.

"Stay put, Rayleen." Stephen was stern with her, noting that he had to be. "I'll see if I can find him. How long has he been gone?"

"Maybe twenty minutes or so. Where would he have gone?" Rayleen paced, her arms wrapped around her toro.

"Home, more than likely. He lives ten minutes from here." Stephen was running for the door and then down the street, heading for Riley's home

Touching the door, Stephen paused. The door was not locked and it should have been. His hand rested on his weapon as he shoved the door open and then entered, searching for Riley. He gave a grim smile as he watched Riley sleeping once more, this time stretched out on his own bed. He sent a text message to Lily and then to Richard.

Richard turned from where he had been watching the team work with Silver, frowning as he pulled out his phone. He sighed. Of course, Riley would go home and cause no end of worry for them all. He sent a text message off to his parents who reassured him that they would head there. When would he be there was their question back to him? He grinned briefly. He was almost through for the day and then would head that way. He knew that Raleigh had headed for Rayleen, worried about that lady.

Raleigh reached to hug Rayleen, finding Rayleen responding. She stepped back to study her and then to study Lily.

"What happened, Rayleen?" Raleigh waited patiently for Rayleen to answer, seeing the worry, stress, and terror in the other lady and knowing somewhat how she felt.

"Riley disappeared without saying anything. I thought that he had been kidnapped again." Rayleen had worked herself up to a high pitch of anxiety and fear by that time.

"Let's find your prayer corner, Rayleen. We need to pray for you." Raleigh wrapped an arm around the other lady, leading her to the living room, with Lily following. "God is here, Rayleen. He has never left you and never will." Raleigh's head was bowed as she prayed for the lady who seemed to have Riley's heart. She just knew that lady would not be leaving their family.

Lily was on her feet a short while later, heading for the door. She opened it to find both Bill and

Andrew, their police chief and a good friend, standing there. She stepped outside, closing the door behind her.

"Lily?   How's Rayleen?"   Andrew was concerned about that lady.

"She's hurting and scared, Andrew. Just like we all were. When she couldn't find Riley, she panicked, something I don't think that she does."

"Not from what we are hearing. Stephen's with him?" Bill looked around, feeling the eyes watching them. "Someone is out there."

"There is. Stephen found signs that someone had been around overnight other than whoever it was who brought Riley here." Lily sighed to herself. "We don't know a lot, now do we?"

"Not enough to solve this. We need that one crucial piece of information and don't have it." Bill shook his head. "I'll head for Riley's. I wish that I wasn't away for the next two weeks."

"You need that vacation time, Bill, as does Cora and your two little ones. You put in a lot of long days." Andrew walked away, needing to be at a meeting that he really didn't want to be at. The meetings with this particular group wee always highly stressful. His steps paused for a moment as a thought crossed his mind. He reached for his phone, sending off a message to Emma and asking her to investigate the group. That had never been done and should have been, he realized.

Bill watched Andrew leave before he too turned.

"I'm heading for Riley's. Stay inside, Lily. I don't want to have to explain to Loch why you disappeared." He grinned for a moment as Lily frowned at him, the mention of her husband reminding her of their own adventure.

Stephen stepped away from the door, allowing Bill inside before he closed the door. Bill could hear quiet conversation and tilted his head before he nodded. Reynold and Rose were there, just as he had expected them to be.

"Where's Riley?" Bill kept his voice low.

"He was sleeping but he's away and getting cleaned up. He hasn't said anything yet but you can see how it affected him. When does it stop, Bill? Does it not stop until one of our friends are killed?" Stephen walked away, angry at the situation, but knowing full well that God was still in control, whether that was how it seemed or not.

Bill nodded himself. He knew what Stephen wasn't asking and had no answers for him. He turned as he heard shuffling footsteps and drew in a deep breath. Whatever Riley had been through? It had changed him. Bill could see it in his face. A hand reached out to stop Riley in his tracks.

Riley's forward motion stopped and for a moment, he felt fear before he recognized Bill's voice.

"You need to talk with me, don't you?" Riley turned towards his office, not seeing his father waiting for him.

<hr>

"I do. Riley, we need to do this now before you have contact with any more people. We need to preserve the integrity of your statement." Bill followed him, taking the water bottles that Reynold was holding out to him with a word of thanks.

"Okay." Riley sank into a chair, not really caring which one it was. "Rayleen? Is she safe?"

"She is. You ended up at her house this morning, did you know that?" Bill grinned at the shocked look on Riley's face.

"I didn't know that. I don't remember a lot from the last few days. It's how he wanted it." Riley sighed. "This is not how the time is to go. And before you say anything, I know that you all felt that way. I've talked in depth with Richard and his team and their spouses. Nothing seems to surprise me any more. Call me a cynic if you like." Riley looked at Bill, seeing the sympathy on his face. "Can we get through the statement? Then I want to find Rayleen."

"And she wants to see you. Lily's with her and will get her to you. Did you know that she's living right now only ten minutes from you? Her home was burned down." Bill was not looking at Riley at that point, missing the shock and then fear that crossed that man's face.

Chapter 25

Riley shook for a moment, the fear that he had felt over the last few days more than he could deal with. He had no recollection of how long it had been and refused to ask. He was afraid for his lady, the lady whom he had acknowledged that he loved deeply in the wee dark hours of his captivity.

"Where do I start, Bill? I have no idea how long it was." Riley rubbed his hands together, feeling cold but not realizing that it was a hot day outside. He just didn't feel the heat for his fear.

"What happened when you were taken?" Bill had his notebook out as well as his laptop open to video record Riley's statement.

"What happened? I can remember calling you and that I wasn't able to leave by either door. Before you arrived, I gather, the doors were broken in and I was tackled to the floor. I fought to escape, Bill. How I fought! I can remember getting the best of one of the men before something landed on my head. It wasn't enough to knock me completely out but enough to subdue me. Two men draped my arms around their shoulders and dragged me from the area that we were fighting in. I was shoved into a vehicle and to the floor of the back seat. I couldn't see anything. That scared me and you know me. I don't scare." Riley's mind drifted back to that day.

Riley had fought to regain his upright position but had been prevented from doing that by the hands and feet that held him down. He was pulled from the vehicle, not able to tell how long it had been but the sense that he had was that it hadn't been that long. He was still in town, what little he could see through his blurry vision.

Shoved into a house, Riley stumbled over a rug and landed on his hands and knees, the fall jarring through an already sore body. He was hauled to his feet and then hauled down a hallway to a room. Shoved into that room, Riley protested at his rough treatment, to no avail. He was forced to stand in the centre of the room.

Riley's body swayed as he tried to keep to his feet. He was unsuccessful in that and landed on the floor, his body hitting hard before his eyes closed. He didn't see the men who stared at him and then at one another. This was not how it was to be. They retreated, heading for the office where they found their employer.

"You have Mr. Ransome ready to speak with me?" The man didn't look up. He fully expected his orders to have been followed to the letter.

"Not exactly. He fought with us. We think that he is injured. He just collapsed." The first man shrank back from the anger on his employer's face. "We tried our best to take him without violence."

"That is no excuse. Revive him. I want him ready to speak to in an hour." The man's hand waved them away.

"How do we do this?" The first man shot a look over his shoulder. "He's not going to wake up."

"No, he's not. Leave him where he is and let the boss see him." The second man walked away, out of the house, and away from it. This had been the final straw, he decided, in whether he stayed employed there or not. He had been moving up the chain of employees and was disliking what he was finding and seeing as he did so.

The first man stood in the room doorway, a shoulder leaning against it. He sighed. This was not how this was to work. Riley was to have come with them peacefully but hadn't. Instead he had fought them. He rubbed at his face, feeling Riley's fists as they had connected with it. It had been a struggle, he knew, and Riley had been winning until the other man had helped take control of the situation.

An hour later, heavy footsteps sounded as the older man stomped towards the room. He didn't find either of the men there and that angered him. His hand reached to unlock the door to the room, hesitating for a moment. For some reason, he was reluctant to enter that room, something preventing it at the moment. He shrugged and shoved at the door, hearing it hit against the wall.

Staring down at Riley, the man's anger grew. Riley was to be on his feet and ready to agree to his terms. He would work for the man in a legal capacity, that the man had determined. Only Riley wasn't awake to agree.

The man's hand found the door, slamming it shut once more and then locking it. He stomped away from that door, searching for any of his employees and not finding any. That was not how it was to be. His phone was out as he summoned those who answered hm. He frowned at his phone. There were a number of men who weren't responding, employees of long standing and that should not be.

He returned to his office to pace, not liking the feeling that he had. Someone was in the room with that man as he called him, and he wanted to know who. Only he was too much of a coward to search himself.

The next morning, three new men were there, rough spoken, rough in the dress, and with evil intentions on their faces. They unlocked the room that held Riley, finding him just rousing as they did so. He was hauled forcibly to his feet and made to stand in one spot. It didn't matter that his body swayed as he tried to keep his balance or that he had to blink repeatedly to clear his vision. That didn't matter to them. All that mattered was the money that they had been promised.

The man stood for a moment in the hallway, his eyes on Riley. He gave an evil chuckle, thinking that he had Riley exactly where he wanted him, down and vulnerable. He just didn't know the character of the man who he would face. It never crossed his mind that Riley would refuse and do so in a gentlemanly fashion.

His footsteps echoed in the nearly empty room. He walked around to stand in front of Riley, his eyes narrowed as he studied the younger man before he nodded. Riley was at the point where he would do anything, he decided. He had ben brought to that point without any of the usual means of drugs or alcohol or shame.

"Mr. Ransome, you will work for me." The man's voice echoed in the room, catching at Riley's attention.

Riley stared at him through blurry eyes. He didn't know the man, he didn't think. Why would he want him to work for him? He had his own work.

Chapter 26

Riley's body continued to sway, the sway becoming increasing harder. At last, he just gave up the fight to stay upright and his body dropped to lie in a crumpled heap on the floor. This shocked the man in front of him. He had expected Riley to be ready to cooperate with him and that just wasn't the case.

His loud and angry footsteps could be heard as he stomped towards his office, his loud and angry voice not covering them. Riley was to be awake and ready to cooperate. This was setting back his plans by hours and that was not acceptable.

The next day found Riley on his feet, unsteady as he was. He rubbed at the back of his head, not sure what he had done that made it so sore. His hand reached for the door knob, finding the door locked. Standing with his back to the door, Riley studied the room and then began a systemic search of any way that he could escape or for anything that he could use for a weapon. Richard had taught his brother well in what to do in situations like this.

Turning as he heard the door unlock, Riley was not surprised to see what he termed as muscle for hire, the two men who had appeared the day before. He watched as they stood to one side so that their employee could enter. Riley kept his emotions from his face, knowing from Richard that he had to. He made no move to approach the man, standing and leaning against a wall. He was ready to defend himself if necessary. His heart was praying for protection, strength, and understanding.

"Well, Mr. Ransome. At last you are on your feet. It's about time. We need to agree to terms." The man stopped in front of Riley, a frown on his face. Riley was not acting as anyone else would have reacted. He was unable to read Riley's face and that frustrated him.

"I don't think so. There are no terms that we could come to an agreement on." Riley stood upright, his arms folding across his chest. "I know who you are and what you do."

"But you see, Mr. Ransome, you will work for me. I need your legal skills." He stared at Riley as Riley continued to shake his head.

The man kept demanding that Riley work for him. Riley would not be released at all. He was now in the man's control and that control meant that Riley was his employee. The man didn't understand that Riley was his own person and that he had God fighting for him. Riley could sense the presence of God's angels around him. None of the men were able to approach him, which seemed to puzzle them.

The man finally turned and stormed from the room. They could hear his loud and angry footsteps as he stomped down the hallway. The two men shared a look and then stared at Riley. It was unheard of in their experience for anyone to refuse to work for the man, not unless they wanted to die. And that didn't happen.

Riley watched as the men slipped quietly from the room and locked the door. He slumped back against the wall, hardly able to stay on his feet, his head dropping in relief. He had survived this encounter. He didn't know if he would survive a second one, and there would be a second one and a third one until either he agreed to work for the man or he was dead. And he would never agree to work for him.

Riley's eyes closed as he swayed from lack of sleep and food. He could not understand why the man had chosen him. He would have lawyers working for him. Riley shoved away from the wall and paced the room over and over. He just didn't understand why.

The next day was a repeat of the day before. Riley steadfastly refused to speak, his eyes not leaving the man in front of him. He could sense and see the anger that was building in him and knew that his days were numbered as they say. Riley was desperately needing food and sleep, neither of which were provided. The man made sure that Riley would not sleep. And food was denied him other than for water. That was not enough to keep Riley going. The man thought that by doing so, he would wear Riley down quickly. He didn't know the character of the man in front of him.

Riley dropped to the floor after that last session. He knew that he could not continue as he was, not and stay alive. His chin dropped to his chest as he sought to sleep, his fatigue to the point that he could not keep awake. He didn't like that feeling but it was what it was. He knew that God was there with him. He had seen the form of a man standing in the front of him as the man had hammered at him, threatening at that point Riley's family and Richard's team. Rayleen was not threatened, which puzzled Riley. He wanted out of there to determine just why.

Late that evening, Riley felt hands on his arms, raising him to his feet. He swayed as he tried to find his balance, something that was hard to do. He squinted at the man beside him, recognizing him as the man who had stood in the gap between himself and his abductor. Riley nodded sightly as the man pointed silently towards the door, his arm now around that man's shoulders.

Riley didn't remember leaving the house or walking from there towards Rayleen. He could not tell Bill where he had been or how long he walked. All he knew was that he was near the lady he loved. Shoved gently down into a deck chair, Riley listened to the man as he cautioned him not to approach the house until he saw Rayleen. That was his duty at that point, to wait for daylight and his lady to appear.

Riley was on his feet as he saw Rayleen, approaching the door and then just sweeping her into a hug. He could feel the questions that she had but he couldn't ask or answer any. He needed to sleep and that was exactly what he did.

Bill looked up at that point, nodding. Riley might not be able to answer many questions for him but he had to ask them any way.

"Riley? Who was it? Who kidnapped you?" Bill waited patiently as Riley's head had dropped when he asked his question.

Riley nodded. Bill did need to know. He just didn't want to say that man's name out loud but he had to. He looked up, seeing Rayleen standing in the doorway. His hand went out as she almost ran to him, wrapped tight in his arms. She had been threatened that last day as had been his family and his brother's team. That scared Riley and not much did.

"Who kidnapped me?" Riley paused, not sure how to phrase what he needed to say. "Who would you suspect, Bill? Would you suspect Moses Laing?"

Bill stared at Riley for a moment before he nodded. There had long been rumours about the man but nothing could ever be confirmed. It just had to be Riley who brought the man down. Laing had hidden himself well behind shell and numbered companies. They all wanted him but had no proof. Not until now.

"Laing? Then you were held at one of his properties." Bill looked down at his notes, knowing that his work had just expanded. "He wanted your legal experience."

"That's what he said. That doesn't make sense, Bill. He has his own lawyers. I don't deal with what his businesses, legal or otherwise are."

"No, you don't. There's a deeper reason for that. I'll pass the name on to Emma and she'll work her magic as she always does to find him. God leads her in those searches." Bill was on his feet, his eyes resting on the couple in front of him. "I don't need to tell you. You need to watch wherever you are, both of you. He'll take Rayleen to make you cooperate. And he'll want you for escaping from him. And I agree with your unspoken thoughts, Riley. It was an angel

---

standing in the gap for you. It was how God chose to protect you."

Chapter 27

Riley studied the lady whom he held tight in his arms. His thoughts had been constant on her, worried that she had been harmed or taken away again. That he could not handle. He sighed. How did he proceed, Lord, was his prayer. Riley didn't want to hurt the lady in his arms but he was well aware that he could.

"Riley? What happened? How did you just appear this morning?" Riley struggled to loosen Riley's grip on her enough to look up at him.

"God. He had an angel standing in the gap for me all the time. The men who tried or wanted to harm me couldn't get near me. The man responsible for this? He couldn't either. God was looking out for me. He was protecting you too from what Bill said. He told me how he just grabbed you and ran from your home." Riley gave a sad smile at the devastation on her face. "It hurts. And it will. Not knowing who did it also doesn't help."

"No, it doesn't. Do we know why you were taken? I wasn't listening to what Bill was asking you. Lily wouldn't let me near the doorway until you had finished." Rayleen was praying that Riley had the answer that would solve whatever it was that day.

"We do know one name. Moses Laing." Riley felt Rayleen stiffen in his arms. "Rayleen? You know him?"

"I do, unfortunately. He's a friend of my father or rather a relative, I think. We need to prove that."

Rayleen had not heard the movements as others joined them in the room. Startled as she felt a hand on her back, she looked around, surprise on her face. "When did all of you arrive?"

Richard grinned at her even as soft laughter filled the room.

"Just now. We've been arriving over the time that you have been here. And yes, we are done training for the day. So that is not something that you need to worry about. Now, how do we do this? I know what I would do but this is yours and Riley's decision on how we proceed." Richard simply bowed his head and prayed for his brother and his lady. He knew they were far from done with their adventure as it was termed. Rayleen was somewhat surprised as he ended his prayer with his usual "I love You" instead of an amen.

"I don't know how to proceed." Rayleen sighed. "This is not what I do, you know. If you asked me about how to treat or track an animal, that I could tell you." She looked thoughtful. "Can we do that with this man? Can we track him using all of our skills?" She looked up at the murmurs in the room.

"We can do that very thing, Rayleen." Timothy was on his feet, heading for Riley's home office, returning with pads of yellow legal paper and pens that he handed out to everyone. "Riley keeps a well-stocked home office." He grinned at her. 'This is how we do it to start. We begin to list everyone whom we know and suspect or not. We list our families, friends, enemies if we know them, co-workers, etc. Once we need to, then we move to paper on the walls."

"Paper on the walls? Really?" Rayleen leaned back against Riley, feeling safe, cherished, and adored without knowing that was how he felt. She knew that she loved and adored the tall man holding her even if it had only been such a short while. Rayleen had always scoffed at the idea of love at first sight, until that was it happened to her.

"We do. We reach out to friends who are investigators and they research and confirm information before it's passed on to the detectives and to us. We usually get the first information. That's just how it works." Richard had picked up the trail of the conversation. "We are not going to walk away from you, Rayleen. That's a given. You're part of our family and group now." He didn't see the surprised look that showed in her eyes for a moment. "We also have others who will work with us, other security teams. Don and I have been friends since we were really small. He has a team of six. And then there's Abe and his team of eight." He grinned as laughter spread through the room, causing Rayleen to frown.

"It's okay, Rayleen." Silver took pity on her. "Abe has a team member, Ian, who offers to fly the couple in danger to somewhere no one would ever find them. So far, I think only one couple took him up on his offer."

"And I pity his daughter when she begins to date." Timothy's grin widened.

"I don't think it will be too bad. He's mellowing now that he's a father but he will keep a close watch on his daughter and all the other girls in their group. They all will." Stephen's voice sounded absentminded. "Riley? Who held you? Do you know?"

"I do. Moses Laing. But somehow, I don't think he's the one that we need to be looking for. He's been too open with what he wanted from me. That was for me to work for him. And I don't understand that at all. Why would he want the skills and experience of a paralegal when he has lawyers working for him?"

"Because if the lawyers are caught, they face disbarment by the legal society as well as jail time. You would lose your license, be barred from practicing as a paralegal and face jail time as well. The consequences of disbarment are not as severe for you as for some lawyer." Reynold was thinking through what he could determine. "I know Laing since we were kids in school. There was also something shifty and devious about him." He smiled as they laughed at his terminology. "We could just not place why."

"And now it's up to Rayleen and me to bring him down, is what you're not saying." Riley sighed. "How do we do it without putting ourselves in more danger? And I don't know that he's the one who abducted Rayleen to begin with. How much have you looked into her employer and those funding him?"

Rayleen's head lifted so that she could watch Riley, finding that man's eyes on hers. She frowned at the look in them, not sure what to think.

"Riley?" Rayleen's voice held both hope and despair.

"We'll look at everyone around us that we can. I have no doubt that John is clear. But someone knows him well enough to know that he has the cottage and that he would offer it to you if something drastic kept you from your own home." Riley spoke the unspoken thought that no one else had wanted to speak.

"Do you think that?" Rayleen's head went down against Riley once more, drawing the attention of the others in the room. "Then, we need to speak with him." Her head raised once more as she heard a familiar voice. "John? You're here?"

"I am, Rayleen." Her employer grinned at her. "And just how are you, Riley? Richard reached out to me earlier today. This is the first that I could break free and come and try and help you all." He accepted the mug of tea as well as the pad of paper and pen. "What are we up to?"

"I'll be okay, John. What are we up to? We are listing everyone that we can think of who may be involved or not. Your name came up just as you came in. We were wondering if someone knew you well enough to know that you would offer Rayleen the cottage."

"That is quite likely. I have not been quiet about the cottage and how I offer it to those needing short-term residence. Rayleen, that fits you. It doesn't make sense that your home was destroyed, other than as a scare tactic to drive you out into the open."

"Only, she didn't do that." Rose spoke up at last. She had made the rounds of everyone in the room, just to pray with them. "And that means that they will go to new lengths to draw her out." She paused, frowning at first Rayleen and then John. "What was her task the day that she disappeared? Had it been planned?"

John was nodding as Rose spoke. She had hit the nail on the head with her questions regarding why Rayleen was out there.

"It wasn't planned, Rose. Not at all. We received word of some raccoon babies in trouble and she went out to try and find them. The last text that I received from her was that she couldn't find any at all and was heading back to the office. That's the last we heard from her until she came home."

Rayleen was nodding.

"That's exactly what happened, Rose. I went out to try and rescue them. Only there wasn't any sign of an animal in trouble or distress. I spent a long time searching. I didn't realize that I was not on my own until the men grabbed me and took off with me." Rayleen was sober as she spoke, her eyes resting on Lily. "Lily?"

"That has answered a question that we had as investigators. We'll talk more." Lily was on her feet, heading for the door and her car. She needed to be elsewhere whether she wanted to be or not.

———

Chapter 28

John looked up at last from the list that he had been composing. He was afraid for his friend, Rayleen, and for Riley. He didn't know the Ransome brothers well other than for their contact at church but he knew them and their reputations. Anything that would harm them reputation had to be considered in the scheme of what was happening.

"Riley? Richard? Reynold? What would be the consequences if your reputations were damaged or destroyed?" John watched the three men closely as their eyes shot to his.

"That's a fair and deep question, John. For me, it's not so consequential as it is for the boys. If Richard's reputation was damaged, then he loses his business and any strides forward that he has made in the security field. For Riley? If his reputation is damaged or destroyed, then any work that he has done in the legal field is suspect." Reynold could see his sons nodding in agreement.

"You're right, Dad." Richard spoke up. "My reputation and the team's reputation are one and the same. If my reputation suffers, so does the team. That makes us suspect in any endeavour we would undertake in the security field. And with Riley, his reputation is what is work is based on as well. People wouldn't trust him if his reputation is suspect."

"I agree, Dad, and I think that is what someone is after. To destroy us somehow. But it would affect your reputation and Mom's as well if we were suspected of being criminals."

"It would, Riley. I have to agree with you, son." Rose spoke up. "And we need to determine who it is before that happens." Rose was on her feet, heading for the door, knowing that Riley would not be rising anytime soon. He was just not letting go of Rayleen and that lady had no intention of moving from him. "Bill? Aren't you supposed to be off duty? And Cora with your two little ones. How nice! Come in. We're meeting and trying to determine who is the culprit other than who Riley named."

Bill grinned at her even as he watched his young son, Michael, run for the living room, intent on finding his friends who were there. Bill had no doubt that his son would be welcomed.

"And have you decided why?" Bill followed Rose, seeing Cora greeting the other ladies.

"We think so." Riley spoke up, waving a paper at Bill. "It's our reputations and that of Mom and Dad's as well."

Bill paused, a thoughtful look crossing his face. He had not considered that, he knew, and wasn't sure if the others had.

"Why would you say that?" Bill found a seat, taking the paper that was passed to him.

"Why not?" Rayleen spoke up. They could hear the anger in her voice. "Someone wants to destroy Riley and his family. And this is one way to do it. If their reputations are suspect, they wouldn't be able to work in this town. And even if they moved to a new town, any investigation into them would show that their reputations were in tatters. How do we prove this and how do we solve this?"

"By a lot of hard work. I know that your friends are at work, Riley and Richard. Emma will be in touch as she finds information for us. You both know that." Bill sighed. "And now that we have it figured out, whoever it is will be coming harder after you, Riley. He'll use you to get to Richard and your parents."

"They will. I just don't understand how Rayleen plays into this. Why was she taken?" Riley turned to John. "John? Have you had any other situations such as what happened that day?"

John shook his head. His team had met and discussed that very idea. There hadn't been another situation such as what Rayleen had faced.

"No, we haven't. That day? It was staged to abduct Rayleen. And I for one would like to know why." John paused, a thought crossing his mind. "What if it was done to make Rayleen look suspect and unstable mentally? Would someone do that and then link her to Riley?"

"That's a good possibility, John. We've been trying to determine that as well but not getting too far." Bill was still frustrated and it came out in his voice.

"We'll get there." Reynold set aside his papers, a sign to his family that he wanted to do something else. "We need to pray for this couple, people. We're all too familiar with what and how to pray." His head was bent as he opened the time of prayer.

An hour passed before Rose was on her feet, Raleigh and Silver with her. They had planned a meal and were heading to finish it off. Rayleen watched them and then shoved at Riley's arms until he let her go. She was on her feet to follow the other ladies, intent on helping them.

Riley watched her walk away before he was on his feet and headed for the outdoors. He needed to pace and couldn't do it inside. He could feel a presence pacing with him that was not visible. He looked up, a thank you sent to God.

Richard watched his brother before he was on his feet, heading to stand on the sidewalk, watching not Riley but around him. He knew that three members of his team were outside as well. Their spouses had arrived during the afternoon, making Riley's house full, but that had not been a problem.

Richard was also well aware that this was a point at which Riley could disappear on them again and never be found. Instead of living the rest of their lives with him, they could be holding a funeral for Riley with no body ever found. He wanted to avoid that.

Riley turned to watch his brother, seeing him in security mode. He sighed. This was not how his life was to be. He had wanted to find a lady to love and adore who would share her life with him. It wasn't supposed to happen this way. He sighed once more. God was in control, he acknowledged. He would never leave either one of them. He had walked the path before them and was walking it with them now. There were times that Riley just could not fathom how God did this for all the people He called His own. It just didn't seem possible to Riley's finite human mind how infinite a God they had.

Richard walked towards his brother, drawing him into a hug before he stood back. He was assessing Riley as he would someone that they were provided protection for and didn't like what he was seeing. The brothers were close and best friends. They had been all their lives even when they took different career paths. They had had few serious squabbles, for the most part able to work through their differences and pray through them. That didn't happen in a lot of families, Riley had to acknowledge.

"What now, Richard? What do we do now?" Riley was at a loss at the moment to know which way to go.

"I can give you all the advice in the world, Riley, and do the same for Rayleen, but it may not help. You know that only too well." Richard grinned at his brother for a moment, a hand up to acknowledge the call from their mother that a meal was ready for them and just when would they be coming to eat before everything was gone.

"Mom will never change. She'll still be doing that for the grandkids." Riley had to grin as well before he sobered. "Let's eat, Richard. Then, everyone needs to get to their homes. It's going to be a long haul with this, I suspect."

"Not as long as you might think. It's going to wear on you and Rayleen. At least with Raleigh and I, we were married and could support one another that way." Richard turned to face the house, an arm across his brother's shoulders. "Emma was in touch. She said that Abe and she would be here in a couple of days."

"She's found something that she needs to verify, I would suspect." Riley sighed again, thinking that was all he ever did. "And I want you in on the meeting as well as Dad and Mom."

"Raleigh and I will be there. My team as well if you want. Don's weighing in. If you need him, he can spring himself and some of his team free to come."

"I know that he will. It's what he does. I'm praying that we don't need to do that." Riley walked up the steps to find Rayleen waiting for him and just hugged his lady. He felt her hugging him back before his head dropped to hers and he began to pray for them both.

Chapter 29

Rayleen paced the cottage the next afternoon. She had to admit to herself that she was bored. Used to working every day with very little time off, Rayleen didn't know what to do with herself. Riley had sent a quick text message that morning just to let her know that he was praying for her and would she have a meal with him that night? She had hesitated to agree, not sure if they should be seen together before she shrugged and agreed. It was what time remained between then and now that she had to fill. A knock at the door had her heading that way, pausing as she looked through the glass.

Her mother stood there, waiting somewhat impatiently for Rayleen to answer. Rayleen backed away to a spot where she could still see her mother but not be seen. Her phone was out as she called Lily.

"Lily? My Mom is at my door. How did she find me? No one outside of our group should know." Rayleen was beginning to panic, not something that she was prone to. She was normally calm, cool, and collected.

"Your mother?" Lily was on her feet, heading for her car. "I'm sending a patrol car. If she leaves, do not go outside. It could be a ploy to have you do just that."

"I know. I won't. I just don't understand how she found me. John would not have told her."

"No, he wouldn't have, not without your permission. Someone who has been watching you has let her know where you are now living. It couldn't be your father. He's still in jail and hasn't spoken to anyone, not even a lawyer."

"That's good, I guess." Rayleen continued to study her mother, a frown appearing on her face. "I don't understand why she would suddenly appear like this." Rayleen sighed before she looked at her phone, scrolling through the applications on it. "There's a location app that I didn't install, Lily. They must have and that is how she found me."

"Don't remove it. Let me have your phone for a day or so and I'll have the techs go over it. We'll find you another phone. Riley needs to keep in touch with you." Lily laughed at Rayleen's grumbling about that before she pulled to a stop at the curb in front of the cottage. "I'm outside now, Rayleen." Lily had sobered by that point. "I'll come and find you once I've cleared it for you to come outside." Lily turned as she heard the patrol car stopping.

Rayleen's mother turned as Lily approached her, not sure why a police officer would be there. Lily's badge was held up for her to read it.

"May I ask why you're here?" Lily moved to stand between the door and the older woman.

"I'm here to see my daughter. She's inside. I know that she is. She will speak with me. I want to know where she's been and why she had her father arrested." The smug arrogance of the woman contrasted greatly with the character of her daughter.

157

"I don't think so. In fact, I know that she didn't do that. For now, the officer right behind you would like you to go with him. You can either go peaceably or we can handcuff you and take you that way. It's your choice." Lily waited, seeing the handcuffs in the officer's hand, which soon were clicked around the woman's wrists as she adamantly refused to leave without seeing her daughter.

Lily watched the patrol officer drive off before she was tapping at the door, finding it opening very quickly. That told her that Rayleen had been just inside the door, watching as her mother was arrested.

"What happened, Lily?" Rayleen rubbed at her cheek. "Did Mom not want to go?"

"No, she didn't. She wanted to speak with you. In fact, she accused you of having your father arrested." Lily shut the door behind her, setting the lock and then heading for the kitchen. She reached for a bottle of water that she opened and handed to Rayleen.

"She what?" Rayleen was shocked at that. "I did no such thing. I saw him at Riley's business but I didn't speak with him. All I said to Bill was that my father was there."

"We know that, Rayleen. We know that you didn't have anything to do with his arrest. He managed that all on his own." Lily paced for a moment. "Why would she accuse you of that?"

Rayleen shrugged. She had no idea why that would have been said. She lifted her eyes to the ceiling, begging God for an explanation, an explanation that just didn't come. She was frustrated at what she was facing, wanting it over so that she could go in with her life. That life meant moving from Elmton, her home town, as much as she hated to even think about that.

"Don't even think of moving, Rayleen. There's a certain good-looking tall gentleman who would just chase after you." Lily grinned at her friend for a moment. "Listen, I need to run. Will you be okay or do you have other relatives that will show up?"

Rayleen shook her head. She had a brother who had walked away from her with her parents. Any other relative that she had? She was no longer in contact with them and that suited her just fine.

"No, I don't think so. I don't have contact with them." She reached for a piece of paper on the kitchen table. "Here. This is a list of them and their friends as far as I could remember. I was working on it this morning." She reached for her phone. "And here's my phone. You have one for me?"

Lily nodded, reaching into her pocket.

"Here. I programmed in what numbers I could. Riley's is in the first contact spot. Send him a text message with the new number and why. He'll have been expecting this." Lily paused for a moment. "How do we do this, Rayleen? How do we keep you and Riley safe? We ask this all the time. To date, we have no good answer for it."

Lily was on a hunt once back at the detachment. She had handed off the phone to a tech and then went looking for Bill.

———

"Bill? I just brought in Rayleen's phone. It had never been searched. She found an app on it that was likely tracking her. And her mother showed up at her door. We had to arrest her when she refused to leave."

"You did? I thought that her phone had been searched." Bill turned from where he had been stirring cream into a mug of coffee. "And her mother?"

"Her mother. She didn't take it well when Rayleen refused to open the door for her. That led to us having to arrest her. What we don't understand is how she found Rayleen."

"The app more than likely. She has another phone?" Bill was concerned about that.

"She does. I found one for her and programmed in all the numbers that she will need. But you know that she and Riley are going to be out there, don't you?"

"I know. We all did that, didn't we?" Bill grinned at Lily. "What else?"

"Rayleen gave me a list of her relatives and what friends of theirs that she could remember. I don't think that we had asked for that and we should have."

"Yes, you are right. We should have. Once more, I thought that we had." Bill ran his hand through his hair. "What else have we missed, Lily? I feel like we have done that."

"I don't know, Bill. I'm going to find Jason and go back over everything once more. Surely we can find something to work with." Lily walked away, leaving Bill staring at the list of names, shock on his face as he saw who was there.

"Andrew? Do you have a moment?" Bill paused at Andrew's office doorway. "Lily just gave me a list of names that Rayleen handed her. Relatives and their friends."

"Something troubling you about them?" Andrew reached for the list, reading through it. "We know a lot of these people, don't we? And most of them are from the wrong side of the line of right and wrong."

"They are. That would explain why Rayleen had a tracking app on her phone. But it doesn't explain why her mother showed up this afternoon at her home."

Chapter 30

Rayleen was both puzzled and angry the next day. She had found a package on her front step and had absolutely refused to move it or even look at it. She recognized her mother's handwriting on it. Rayleen had called Bill, able only to leave voice mail for him. She paced around the outside of her house, studying the gardens and the surrounding areas, knowing full well that she had no idea what she was looking for.

The sound of a closing car door had her cautiously peering around the corner of the house before she walked towards Jason. He would do, she decided, if Bill was unable to make it.

"Jason? You're here? Where's Bill?"

Jason grinned at her even as he saw the ravages of what she was going through on her face.

"He's in court today and tomorrow. I'm picking up for him. He said something about a package?" Jason paused beside her, his senses alert that something was amiss.

"There is. On the front porch. And my name is in my Mom's handwriting. If she's in jail, how did it get here?" Rayleen refused to move any closer to the cottage.

"I see. Let me take a look. I have a tech on the way as well." Jason walked towards the cottage, stopping on the front deck to study the package. He didn't like it one bit, not after what had happened to her own home. He turned and walked away, a hand out to draw Rayleen further from the building. "We need to stay clear of that, Rayleen. Given what happened at your home, I am calling in the bomb squad. And no, it is not overkill."

Jason watched closely as the bomb squad leader approached him, the box in his hands. That man was puzzled by what was inside.

"Jason? What is this? There was no bomb. I'm glad that you called us in anyway, given what had happened to her home." James set the box on the hood of Jason's car. "This is not making sense to me, but it might to you."

Jason stared down into the box, a frown deepening on his face. He felt a presence beside him before he heard Rayleen exclaim.

"What has she done? These things are not mine. What is she up to?" Rayleen backed away from the box, hitting a male body as she did so, that male just wrapping her into his arms.

Riley had been heading home with his paperwork, determined to work from home. At the activity that he saw at Rayleen's home, he had simply pulled over to the curb and came to find her, wrapping her against him.

"Rayleen? What is this?" Riley's voice sounded in her ears even as she leaned harder back against him.

"I have no idea. The box had Mom's handwriting on it but what's inside has nothing to do with me. I don't understand." Rayleen's face was sober as she looked at Jason whose gaze was shifting between Rayleen and the box.

Jason sighed. This was not how it was to be. Whatever was in the box should be explained away by Rayleen. Only that lady was unable to do just that. "What can you tell me about any of these?"

Rayleen shook her head. She just refused to approach the box, feeling such a sense of evil and danger.

"I don't recognize anything, Jason. Please don't make me look in it again." She was begging and they all knew it.

"I won't, but I will be showing you pictures. How be you head back into the cottage and lock yourself in there. And yes, Riley can go with you. In fact, that's like a very good idea that the two of you are together. It makes it easier to keep track of you." Jason turned back to the box and the tech who had appeared, his conversation too quiet for Rayleen to hear.

Riley nudged her towards the cottage, watching as Richard and Don approached. This ws not good, he decided, that the two of them were there.

Richard's face was grim as he watched the activity around the building. He shared a look with Don who in turn had looked around.

"What happened, Richard? Do you know?" Don headed for the house, Richard matching him stride for stride.

"No, I have no idea. But I am sure that Rayleen will be vocal as she tells us. She tends to be like that when she is scared."

"Or else she will withdraw totally." Don tapped at the door before he opened the door. He frowned as he didn't hear any sounds of anyone inside. "Richard? Riley and Rayleen just entered here, didn't they?"

"They did." Richard's face grew even grimmer as he paced through the house and then outside. He drew in a breath of relief. Rayleen and Riley were seated on the back deck, Rayleen wrapped tight in Riley's arm. That man was not letting go of his lady.

Rayleen peeked around Riley at Richard before she was frowning at him and then at Don. Don she had met over the course of her work.

"Richard? Don? You're here? Don't tell me. Bill or Jason called you in." Rayleen sounded disgruntled at that.

Richard grinned at her even as he caught Don shaking his head at her.

"Not at all. We just had to come. God told us that we had to." Richard found a seat. "Talk to me, Rayleen. What happened just now?"

Rayleen almost spit her words at him as she explained. The three men were not taken aback at the vehemence in her words. It was to be expected. She was being pushed to her limit and likely by this point had reached it.

"You didn't recognize anything in the box?" Don was making notes, knowing that his team would want to work this angle.

"Not a thing. Other than recognizing my Mom's handwriting on the outside, I don't recognize anything in it. What is she doing?"

"What you are feeling? The fear, anger, whatever else? That's what she wants you to feel. The uncertainty of when someone will strike at you two again plays on your mind." Don was very open with how he spoke to the couple. "We've been through something similar, Rayleen, and can confirm that we felt all of those emotions and more."

"I know. I just wish that it hadn't happened. We have no explanation as to why I was taken in the first place. John has tried to figure it out as have my team members. None of us know why. And that is not helping to keep our team together."

Don pointed at her, stopping her words. She stared at him, wondering why he had done that.

"If your team splinters and breaks up, what happens to your work?" Don's question stopped Rayleen from saying anything eyes.

Her mouth opened and closed before she was reaching into her jeans pocket for her phone and sending that question to John. He would appear at her home, she had no doubt. Had Don just found the link that they were missing?

____

Chapter 31

Walking around to the back of the cottage, John hesitated before he approached the deck. There were more people there than he expected. Richard stood beside him. He had been walking around the property, watchful for anything out of the ordinary, when John arrived.

"We had friends drop in unexpectedly, John. Abe and Emma Finlay information that they wanted to bring to Riley and Rayleen." Richard had not read the material yet, setting his copy to one side. He planned on reading through it in the next little while.

"I see. I know Emma through work. I have never met her in person." John looked up as he heard someone clear his throat.

"That would be my wife. I'm Abe." Abe reached to shake John's hand. "I hear that you may have information for us."

"I might. We're meeting out here?" John watched as Rayleen noticed him, a frown on her face changing to a hesitant smile.

"We are. For now, we plan to share a meal and then a time of prayer. That is badly needed." Abe knew only too well how they couple felt to some extent. He and his team and many friends had faced what they called adventures, even though they were life and death struggles.

"That is good. We need to do that. My team has been coming in early to meet and pray for Rayleen and

Riley. It is only God who will get them through the next while." John walked up to the deck, reached to hug Rayleen and then shake Riley's hand. He studied the couple and had to agree with his wife that they were indeed a couple. He could see the glances that they were shooting at one another, hoping that the other was not watching them. John remembered only too well what young love was like and prayed for his friends that they would indeed survive what they were going through to admit their love for one another.

Two hours later, Richard reached for his paper work. He had found a seat beside Riley, needing to be close to his brother.

"Riley? Talk to me. Tell me what you found." This was common for the brothers to react to one another like this. Both were deep thinkers, pondering what they were learning before they spoke.

"I don't like it. Laing is not the only one involved, I know that much. But who else is involved? That we don't know as yet. Kat sent on her family trees for both of us again, or as much as she would release. Emma said that she was passing them on to Bill as well. Darci has weighed in with her profile. I would suspect that she is spot on once more." Kat was the wife of one of Abe's team members and had a program where she could trace family trees for investigators. Darci was the wife of Abe's cousin, Doug, who was the emergency task force lead in their town. She was also a retired forensics psychologist who had been forced to retire from that after being harassed by a police officer and her supervisor. She did profiles for friends now even as she ran an arts and crafts store.

———

Richard nodded. He had come to the same conclusion as his brother. Laing was involved but they had no idea how involved he was other than wanting or rather demanding that Riley work for him. That was not about to happen, both brothers knew.

"I know what you mean, Ry. Raleigh had a thought. What if working for Laing was just a front for him, to try and make him seem legitimate?" Richard's hand went up as Riley opened his mouth to speak. "Think about it for a moment. Almost everyone we could speak with would say that Laing is crooked. We know that. We just don't know why he went after you other than what we determined last night. Destroy our reputations and they destroy our lives. And who would want that badly enough to hire Laing to do what he did?"

Riley was listening intently to his brother. His eyes found Raleigh who was nodding as Richard spoke.

"You may be on to something there, Raleigh. I didn't get the sense that Laing was really in earnest, even though that was how he tried to portray it. He had an ulterior motive in there. I for one want o know what that was." Riley reached for Rayleen's hand as she paused beside him, pulling him down beside him on the swing. "Rayleen? What would you say to that?"

Rayleen studied him and then Raleigh. She found John watching her intently, a look on his face that said he agreed with the others.

"I would say then that we are on to something. But how do we prove it? Who would be backing him in this? Emma?" Rayleen turned towards the other lady. "What have you found out?"

"That Laing is indeed a criminal. I have passed all that information on to the appropriate detective. But you are correct. He is being used. I haven't determined yet by whom but I will. We are working through layers of aliases and companies to do that." Emma sighed as her phone chimed and she was on her feet to answer another call for another investigation. She was tired, she decided, and desperately needed a break to go find her eagles.

Abe watched her walk away before he was motioning to Richard and Don. The three men walked away, Rayleen watching them and desperately wanting to know what they were planning. That they were planning something was obvious.

"Rayleen?" John's voice brought her attention back to him. "What can we do for you? I know that you're all working through this, the detectives are, and so are your friends. We are praying for you. But how do we be the hands and feet of God on earth for you and Riley?"

Rayleen shrugged. She had no idea. She was on her feet and walking away, leaving everyone staring after her.

Two hours later, Rayleen returned to the back deck, finding everyone gone but Riley. She thought that she was on her own but he had not left her. She walked into his hug, holding on tighter that she normally would have.

"Okay, sweetheart?" Riley's term of endearment sparked the tears that she had been trying to hold back. He simply held her as she wept, his own tears wetting her hair. The lady that he loved was hurting and he could not make it better for her.

"Thank you, Riley, for being who you are." Rayleen looked up at him, a frown as she saw the look in his eyes. "Riley?"

"I love you, Rayleen. There. I've said it and put it out there for you." He gave a soft smile, seeing the softening on her face. "I hadn't meant to say that as yet."

"And why not? Do you know how long I have prayed for someone like you? I love you too. I just thought that it was too soon." Rayleen was not surprised when his head bent and he kissed her.

"I did too but obviously God didn't. I have a meal waiting for us, and then we pray. We'll talk, sweetheart. We'll talk, I'm not walking away from you, not ever. Not if I can help it." Riley kissed her again before he turned her to the table and seated her. His hands reached for her as he prayed not just for their meal but for their protection as well.

Chapter 32

Rayleen had watched Riley walk away at last, a good night kiss delivered by the tall handsome man who had claimed her heart. She tidied up the kitchen and then stood in what she was using as an office. She nodded to herself, liking how John had laid out the rooms. He had put thought into them.

Hearing a tapping at the door, Rayleen froze. No one should be there, she decided, before she crept slowly toward the front door. She frowned before she opened it, only to be swept into a mother hug by Rose.

"Rose?" Rayleen was not sure why the older lady was there but she was glad that she was.

"Riley called me as he left. He thought that you needed a mom and that your mom wasn't here. He asked if I could and would step in. Of course, I would. I think that you're going to be part of our family any way." Rose smiled at the younger lady as she struggled with tears, a mother prayer whispered for her.

"I am, I think." Rayleen frowned as Rose laughed. "That's not how I meant that to come out. We do love one another, Rose. We just admitted that."

"We could see how you two were feeling towards one another. Welcome to the family." Rose hugged her again. "Now, what can I do for you?"

Rayleen shrugged, not sure what to say. Her own mother should be there but wasn't.

"Mom was never there when I needed her. I often wondered about that but then shrugged it off, thinking it was just her." Rayleen studied Rose. "Rose, can I ask you something?"

"Of course, you may. What would you like to know?" Rose's arm around Rayleen drew her back to the office. "I like this cottage. It's you."

"It is but I'll be rebuilding my home, I think." Rayleen didn't see the look that Rose directed her way. "About what Riley and me are going through. What are your thoughts?"

"That's a good question, Rayleen. Let's sit and we'll talk about it. I suspect that Reynold will show up at some point, if you want him to."

Rayleen shrugged. It was not how she thought a father should act but it was who this family was.

"It's okay. I'm puzzled. First, why take me? What was the reason or purpose in that? And how did Riley end up there?"

"Riley can't tell us. He just was driving around that day and felt his car turning that way. He says it was God who sent him that way. I would tend to agree with him." Rose smiled gently at Rayleen. "God can and will do that, Rayleen. We've seen it time and again with our young friends. You need to hear their stories."

"I have heard them. They are incredible. I can see how God would work that way. Riley is insistent that he saw a man in the shadows in my room, standing guard at the door. Does God do that?"

"He does, Rayleen. Oh, how He does. We have heard it time and again. We have hosted many missionaries over the years and that is a common theme. God has provided His angels to keep watch over them. Riley is also insistent that there was an angel with him."

"I know. I understand that, I guess. It's hard as humans to really understand. But who do you suspect?" Rayleen was praying that Rose would have an answer for her.

"Who do I suspect? Laing for one. But he has deep roots in this town. Unless you know his history, you don't know who all he is connected to. Emma is finding these individuals and confirming who needs to be arrested. That is an ongoing task for her. I know that she has been called into an urgent investigation but she hasn't dropped yours. Her team will work it as they already are and she will keep a finger on it. She never loses sight of any investigation that she has in the works."

"That's what Riley and Richard and yes, Don, all said. I don't know how she finds what she does." Rayleen gave a small smile as Rose laughed. "I know. She can't explain it. But who else do you suspect?"

"That is again a good question." Rose thought through the town that she had been born and raised in and the people in it. She began to name names, watching as Rayleen scrambled to list them.

"Them? I wouldn't have." Rayleen was shocked at some of the names that Rose was listing.

———

"No, they keep themselves well hidden. I grew up with them as did Reynold. We know their character from when they were small. They haven't changed, just hidden what they do. Now, how do we do this? Do we work with Richard's team or do we go to Bill, Jason and Lily? Or even Andrew?"

"Let's work it on our own. Richard said that his team is willing to meet again tomorrow, Saturday and all. They want this over for us. He's arranging for us to meet at his home." Rayleen was slightly disturbed at that, thinking that the team needed to be with their spouses and families, not working this.

"It's what they do, Rayleen. It's who they are. They want this over for you and Riley so that you can go on with your lives. And don't even think about running. Riley would come after you and that means every single one of us would be trailing after you two. Can you just see the stream of people?" Rose began to laugh, startling Rayleen for a moment before she imagined that and also broke down in laughter, tears streaming down her face as she did so.

Reynold paused in the doorway. Rose had been on her feet to let him in. His hands held bags of food for the three of them. His puzzled look turned from Rayleen to Rose, who took pity on him and described just how all of them were trailing after Riley who was running after Rayleen to stop that lady from leaving town. He began to laugh, having to set the food down before he was wiping at his own eyes.

"I can just see the crowd that we wold have. And we would bring in our friends from outside of town, now wouldn't we?" Finally sobering, Reynold passed out their meal that he had brought them, courtesy of Andrew's Aunt Ev who had a favourite diner. "Let's eat, ladies. Then we will pray. And then I want to know what you two have been up to." His grin at Rayleen had her hands stopping for a moment as she reached for the styrofoam container of food. He looked so young and so much like his sons. She shifted her gaze to Rose and found that lady nodding at her in agreement that yes, Reynold did at that moment resemble his sons.

Chapter 33

Four days later, Riley stared down at the package that sat on his desk. He didn't remember receiving it and his secretary hadn't either. He was worried. It was a small package with his name and address handwritten on it. There was just no stamp or courier label on it to say how it got there. Riley reached to pull up his security feed, finding it off line.

"That's par for the course." Riley was muttering to himself, jumping as he felt a hand on his shoulder.

Paul and Joshua from Don's team stood on either side of him. He had not heard them enter but knew that Amy, his secretary, would have sent them his way. She knew the members from the three teams only too well.

"Riley? What's with that parcel?" Joshua broke the silence that seemed to hang in the air.

"I have no idea. It's just here. We looked at the security feed and it's down." Riley turned to Paul. "I have it up on the computer in the security room. Go and see what you can discover. Joshua, we need to open this. I don't know that I am ready to call in Bill or whoever just yet."

Paul nodded as he had expected Riley to do just that. Richard would have or would he? Probably not, but then he was not Riley. Riley didn't think through all the scenarios that Richard and everyone else on a security team would.

"Let me look at it first, Riley." Paul's hand landed on top of the parcel to prevent Riley from picking it up. "We need to do that. If you don't let me, then I'll call in whoever it is that I need to." Paul was not backing down from Riley. He couldn't. No one knew what was in that parcel, whether it meant harm to the other man or not.

Riley stared at him before his eyes slid closed. Of course, there might be danger in it. He just wasn't thinking straight. Too many nights with little to no sleep were affecting how he thought and reacted.

"Go ahead, Paul. Check it out. I'll make us coffee. I'm sure that we'll need it."

Paul could hear Riley speaking with Amy before his voice died away. He heard the front door open and close and peeked out. Amy had left. Probably a good move on Riley's part, he thought.

His attention went to the parcel as he reached into a pocket. They all carried packets of latex gloves, just as a matter of habit. He snapped on a pair before his phone was out and he snapped photos of the packet and then set the phone where it would video tape him opening it. Like Riley had observed, he didn't feel anything evil about it and that both surprised and worried Paul.

The pocket knife in his hand was suspended over the packet for a moment before Paul sliced through the end of the packet. He frowned. Nothing overt seemed wrong but it was still concerning. He dumped out the contents, frowning even harder. Paul turned as he heard both Joshua and Riley approaching him.

Riley stood beside his friend, staring down at the material on the desk. He too was puzzled at not feeling any danger. There should have been.

"Paul? What do we have?" Joshua spoke from the other side of Riley. The two men had positioned themselves on either side of him, ready to take him down or away if that was necessary.

"It's puzzling, Joshua." Paul moved the material around with the end of his pocket knife. "Photos. A ring. A business card. A thumb drive." He turned to look at Riley. "Who would be sending you this?"

"I have no idea." Riley reached for a pen to snag the ring. "This is a wedding band. I'm not married. And neither is Rayleen. So, whose is this?"

"That's a good question." Joshua reached for it with a gloved hand. "There are no initials or date inside. What are all the photos?"

"That's a good question too, Joshua. Riley, I've spread them out. Do you recognize anyone in them?"

Riley studied the photos before he shook his head. His phone was out to snap copies of them.

"I don't know them but Mom and Dad might. I recognize buildings and parks from town. What's on the thumb drive?" He reached for his, his hand stopped in midair by Paul's. "Pall?"

"We're not opening it on one of your computers, Riley, just in case. You know why. Where can we go to open it?" Paul waited patiently for Riley to respond.

Riley sighed. He had wanted to keep Richard out of any more of his trouble but it seemed as if that wasn't happening. He turned as he heard Rayleen's voice.

"Rayleen? What are you doing here?" He reached to hug his lady.

"Looking for you." She walked out of his hug towards the table, eyeing the photos. "Why do you have photos of Dad's family?"

"These people are your family?" Paul shared a look with Joshua. This was not what they had expected to hear.

"They are. And that ring? That was his mother's wedding band. I can vaguely remember seeing it on her finger. I didn't see her much. For some reason, he would not let me." Rayleen wasn't upset at what she saw, just resigned. "How did you get them, Riley?"

"There was a packet put on my desk sometime this morning after I arrived. Amy wasn't in yet. There's a thumb drive as well."

"And you need a computer to open it on. Come on, Riley. Lock up your building. You're not getting any work done today, are you? Take me to the cottage. We can use mine. I have a laptop that I don't use. We can use it to open that drive." Rayleen walked away, thinking that she had solved the problem but instead she had just created a new one as to why Riley was receiving information on her family.

"You heard the lady, guys. Let's go before she disappears on us and beats us to her home." Riley watched as Paul gathered the material and then locked the building. He felt watched, the person watching him almost too close to him. He looked around, not seeing anyone but knowing that someone was out there.

Joshua waited beside Riley as Paul stopped beside Rayleen. This is when the couple could very well disappear and they wanted to prevent that at all costs.

"Let's move, Riley. We need to get you out of here." Joshua almost shoved Riley towards his truck, reaching for the keys. "Both of you in the back seat. I'm driving. Paul will follow us."

The two men watched as a car pulled out behind Paul, following them almost too closely. It had been that close to the couple disappearing for good.

Rayleen twisted on her seat, staring out of the back window. She saw Paul behind them and then caught a glimpse of the car behind him. She sighed. Of course, that man would be there.

"That car? It belongs to the man who abducted me. He's still around, isn't he? When we will be free of him?"

Joshua shot her a quick glance, seeing Riley pulling out his phone and making the call that they all prayed would find the man under arrest. They watched as police lights shone behind the man and the car was pulled over. They had to keep driving but they were confident that the man would be arrested and would not be free to come after the couple again. The only worry was who else was out there that had been employed by him. Paul was certain that the man had someone on his payroll who would continue to watch the couple and try and abduct them once more.

<hr>

Chapter 34

Riley stood with an arm wrapped around Rayleen. Instead of heading for her place, Richard, upon hearing what Riley had received, had asked that they come to his training building. That way, there was a computer that they could use without any danger of it being tampered with. Richard also wanted to ensure that his brother and his lady stayed safe. He had no other way of doing that without actually being around them. Even then, he could not guarantee their safety.

Rayleen watched carefully as Paul and Joshua along with Timothy and Silver sorted out the material before Paul and Timothy headed for a computer with the disk drive. She had been assured that she would be able to see the material at the same time as Riley. She had not been pleased that she had to stand back but Riley's arm around her kept her in place.

Riley knew that the lady he loved was angry and troubled. He turned her away from the conference room and towards the reception area, watching as she paced. All he could do at that point was pray for her and he didn't know it that would be enough.

Richard headed away from the training building towards the office building, the head of the team in for training striding beside him. Peter was a good friend of his. That team hadn't really needed the training but as Peter put it, they needed to stay current with their training and what was out there. Richard had always been up to date on everything security related.

"What's going on with Riley?" Peter watched the younger man for a moment, his hand on Richard's arm to stop him.

"He's in the midst of one of those adventures that we all seemed to think that we had. We're nowhere near finding out why or who the head person is at this point." Richard stood where he could watch his brother, seeing the turmoil that Riley was trying had to hide. "It's different when it's not you and it's a family member."

"Who's the lady?"

"The lady? A lady by the name of Rayleen." Richard turned at a sound from Peter. "Peter?"

"What's her last name?" Peter could hardly get his words out.

"Randell." When Peter didn't speak, Richard shot a quick glance towards Rayleen, finding her standing and staring at nothing. "Peter?"

"That's my cousin. My cousin, Rayleen. We haven't seen her in like twenty years. Her father cut all ties with his family. We could never understand or find out why. Gramps wanted to search for Rayleen and was in the process of hiring a private investigator at that time. Grams stopped him. She wouldn't say why but I know that she had been really hurt by something Rayleen's father said to her." Peter moved forward, hearing Richard's footsteps behind him. He paused beside Riley, nodding at that man before his attention focused on Rayleen.

"Rayleen?" Peter spoke her name, watching as she froze for a moment before she turned.

Rayleen turned as someone different spoke her name, a man whose voice sounded somewhat familiar. She frowned at him, thinking that he looked familiar.

"Rayleen? What a relief! Do you know how long it's been that we've lost you?" Peter moved towards her, stopping just short of her.

"Do I know you?" Rayleen struggled with her memory, searching Peter's face and seeing someone familiar and known to her. "I do know you. Peter?" She sobbed as she threw herself at her cousin, their tears mingling.

Riley stared at the two and then at Richard.

"Richard? Care to explain?" Riley was confused, to say the least.

"I can. That's her cousin, Peter. He hasn't seen her is quite some time." Richard turned away, his emotions getting the best of him.

Peter stepped back for Rayleen, his hands on her arms.

"Rayleen? You have a whole huge family looking for you."

"I do? I didn't know that. All I know is that Dad cut off all contact with all of them. Didn't they try to find us?" Rayleen was confused.

"They did at first. Then Grams confronted your dad, I think. We don't know what was said to her but she refused to let any of us look for you. That hurt her and Gramps." Peter turned to Riley. "Riley? Your lady?"

"She is but I don't understand." His further words were cut off as Silver appeared. "Silver?"

"We've looked at the thumb drive. We need you to look at it, Rayleen." Rayleen was away from the men, Riley on her heels, before anyone could stop her.

Peter walked to where Richard was waiting, shaking his head. It had to be God, he decided, to bring his team there that week.

"What have you discovered, Richard?"

"Not what we want. We're missing a piece of the information, although with what was given to Riley, we might just have it." Richard shook his head. He still had trouble wrapping his mind around the fact that Peter and Rayleen were related.

"We can stay if you need our help to research anything. Our wives are away on a vacation for the next three days. They decided to take the time while we were away." Peter waited patiently for Richard to respond.

"That would be great. You can help fill in the blanks on your family." Richard pointed towards the conference room. "Find your team and bring them in. I have copies of everything that we've discovered so far up until today. And I know that Bill, Jason, or Lily will be around at some point. I don't think they'll be too happy that Riley refused to share what he received."

———

185

"It was meant for him and Rayleen. It's not threatening. There is no way that they can take that. Provide them with copies and what you determine." Peter walked away at that point, looking for his team.

Richard had nodded before he looked around. The team members' spouses had shown up. He reached to hug his wife, not saying anything. He felt a hand on his shoulder before his father moved past them, his mother following.

Chapter 35

Three days later, from the safety and security of Riley's arms, Rayleen watched as Peter and his team drove away. She was saddened at that but knew that he had reached out to her extended family. There was great joy that he had connected with her but also fear on their part for what she was facing. He had promised to arrange a dinner or something, he grinned as he said that, for her to reconnect with the family. Only she was too afraid to do that at this time.

Riley hugged his lady, knowing that she was afraid but also happy if there could be such a combination. They had not had much chance to talk about where they went as a couple, but it would come, he knew.

"What do we do now, Rayleen?" Riley had been involved deeply in the research, using his connections as he could to try and prove facts. That had happened, for which Rayleen was grateful.

"I don't know, Riley. I really don't know. I haven't heard from Bill in the last few days." Rayleen was concerned about that.

"He's been away. Wesley's wife is sick and he's been in Oak City with him. He's back tomorrow. I spoke with Jason early today. He's working through what Emma has sent them. He needs to meet with us." Riley frowned at the dark look that covered his lady's face. "Rayleen?"

"That's all we seem to do is talk. When will it end?" Rayleen knew that she was tired and stressed and that was affecting her emotions. "I'm sorry."

"Don't be sorry. It's how you're feeling. I can take that. What I couldn't take was if you walked away from me or died." Riley put his love out there for her.

"I know, Riley. I feel the same. Only it's too soon, isn't it?" She felt his arms tighten around her.

"Not really. For now, let's set this aside and go out for a meal. We can head for Ev's diner. I'm told that Avery, Andrew's cousin, is working tonight. That will provide some sense of safety for us."

Rayleen nodded, knowing that they had to put themselves out there. Only she was afraid to do so. That's when something dire and horrible could happen, she decided.

"I guess. I don't like this, Riley."

"I know that you don't." He looked around as Richard spoke from behind him. "What did you say, Richard?"

"I asked if you two wanted to go on a double date. If not, we'll just head for the same spot." Richard grinned at Rayleen as she turned.

"I guess if it's okay with Rayleen." Riley was dumbfounded as Rayleen broke free from his arms and approached Raleigh.

"Let's leave these two to figure it all out. Are you game?" Rayleen grinned at Raleigh who began to laugh.

"I'm game. Let's head out." Raleigh felt Richard reach for her hand as she saw Riley reaching for Rayleen. "I like this, you know. Both the brothers have their ladies. Riley has been missing that."

Riley began to laugh, even as he shuddered at the eyes watching them.

"I have been but no more. God's timing is perfect."

Late that night, Riley stood in the darkness of his living room, watching as two men snuck around his house, trying to find a way in. He sighed as he reached for his phone. This was not how his evening was to end, not at all. He was glad that his lady and Richard's got along.

Two hours later, Riley finally settled down in his desk chair. He needed to sleep but he also needed some God time. He reached for his Bible, searching for all the verses that he could which would bring peace and comfort to him. His head then bowed as he prayed and waited patiently for God's touch. It could come in minutes or it could take hours.

Rayleen roused in the early morning hours, sensing that God was waking her. She was on her feet and dressed, heading for the back door and slipping through it. She ran for the back yard, cutting through the yards behind her until she reached Riley's street. Rayleen ran for his back deck, seeing a light on in the kitchen. She tapped quietly at the door, finding Riley first staring at her in shock and then drawing her inside before he locked the door.

"What happened?" Riley reached for his phone and called Jason whom he knew was working and asked him to check Rayleen's home. She was safe with him although he did not know why she was there.

"God. He told me to leave the cottage and come to you." Rayleen paced, knowing that something was going on at the place that she now called home. "I'm scared, Riley. Who is doing this to us? Did we even make any progress over the last few days?"

"We did. We sent everything on to friends who are investigators as well as to Emma and her team. Emma was in touch just a bit ago. She has some information that she needs to confirm and then she and Abe and his team are heading this way. She's bringing Doug and Darci as well."

"Okay. I don't know these people but you do." Rayleen smirked at him for a moment as he stared at her, forgetting to close his mouth for a moment.

Riley just reached to kiss her before he was moving to pour their coffee. He had a feeling that it was going to be a long day. He yawned and rubbed at the back of his neck. Riley didn't like the feeling that he had, that something had happened at her home.

"Rayleen? You're sure that you're okay?" Riley turned to face her, finding her frowning at him.

"I am, Riley. I am now that I'm with you." Rayleen walked away, studying the home that she knew would be hers at some point. She liked it. It was a home that she could live in and raise a family, if God willed that for them.

———

Riley followed her, not sure what she was thinking.

"Rayleen? Talk to me? You're troubled." Riley finally stopped her in her tracks and just hugged her.

"I am okay. But we need to solve this. And I think it has to be in the next few days or we won't survive. When is Emma coming?" Rayleen watched as Riley muttered before he pulled out his phone.

"They're heading here today as is Don't team. Your cousin's team is heading here as well. And Richard will be here." Riley looked up in surprise as she laughed.

"You're going to have a full house. Do you have enough food to feed them all?" Rayleen hugged him and then headed for the door, peeking out to see Jason standing there. "Jason? What was wrong at the cottage?"

"A lot. It's good that you left, Rayleen. They managed to break in through a window. We caught them in the act of trying to plant devices to track you and listen in on you." Jason was angry that this had happened.

"I see. God was at work, Jason. He spared me being hurt. If I had been there, I would have disappeared. That is true, isn't it?" Rayleen was challenging him.

"It is, Rayleen. How do we keep you safe?" He looked at the two as they began to laugh hard.

<hr>

"It's okay, Jason. We have four security teams heading our way today. Want to join us?" Riley grinned at his friend.

192

The women on Richard's team cornered Rayleen and Raleigh, pointing towards the sunroom. Finding seats, Silver shared a look with Naomi.

"We need to cover you two in prayer. I know that we already are but this has to be concentrated on today. This is ending soon, Rayleen, and this is where it always gets so dangerous." Silver was adamant on that.

"I know. I've heard your stories and the stories of your friends, including Madigan and Silas and Andrew and Phoebe. Madigan and Silas are on their way over, she said." Rayleen looked at the other three ladies. "I want this over. Riley loves me and I love him. We want to go on with our lives. And I have extended family that I want to get to know again. And I won't go near them yet."

"No one is blaming you, Rayleen. They blame whoever it is." Naomi spoke up. "We weren't blamed when we went through stuff."

"Such an elegant term there, Naomi. Stuff." Raleigh laughed, watching as Riley peeked in to watch his lady.

"It describes it well. Now, what did we really learn?" Naomi raised her head at last.

"That my father kept me from my family. And I want to know why. Can anyone tell me that?" Rayleen looked around as she felt someone near her. Emma and the lady introduced as Darci found seats. "Emma?"

"I can tell you why, Rayleen. It was over a house. He wanted the family home and his parents weren't ready to leave it. They still live there. I spoke with your grandparents. They were saddened when he took offence at their refusal to give it to him and cut contact with them. They are so looking forward to seeing you again."

"Over a house? That's it?" Rayleen was shocked. "I don't get it. He had a home. What was so special about that one?"

"No one is quite sure but your grandfather thinks that your father wanted to look richer than he was. His house didn't do that while your grandparents' one did. It has been in the family for years." Emma turned to Darci. "Darci? Did we ever come to a conclusion if that was the case?"

"We did, as you well know, Emma. The one really after Rayleen is not connected to her family. That's a side issue. What we have determined is that the ones after Rayleen are also after Riley. Somehow they connected the two of them when Riley appeared at the store. They thought that he was there to rescue her."

"Only he wasn't. I don't get how they thought that. They had me in their control for two months I think by that time. Wouldn't Riley have appeared before if he knew where I was and was intent on rescuing me?"

"That is the case, Rayleen." Emma was nodding. "The men who are in custody including the store owner are not the brightest of people. They are just employees of someone else. They stepped out of line when they took Riley captive. That was not to happen,". Emma could explain nothing more as that was part of the investigation that Bill and Jason were working on.

"I see. So, he was taken in error. But why take him captive and try and make him work for them? Do we know shy?"

"We do but I can't say. Bill or Jason is working on that. It's part of their investigation. They'll speak with you when it's time. Now, what else can we do for you?" Emma reached to hug Rayleen.

"I don't know, Emma. Thank you for coming. We have so many here today. I feel overwhelmed with all the help that has been coming through."

"And it will continue until this is over." Darci leaned forward. "It's going to end in the next few days, Rayleen. This is where your faith will be sorely tested and you will want to run away and hide. Don't do that. Stay and fight. If you run, Riley will run after you. That leaves you both vulnerable to whoever it is. And if he or she has you in his or her control, this time you won't survive. That's a guarantee. You escaped many times on him, more than you likely even know about. He or she has lost face with others and need to reclaim it. You will be victims that we don't want."

"I know, Darci. That's what scares me. We don't know who other than it's someone from town.

Do you have a name?" Rayleen was praying that she did. She looked in shock and then horror as Darci named someone. "That person? Oh no! We'll never get away from him."

"But you see, you have God on your side. You will survive. You may not like that you will be in danger or even injured." Emma knew from experience what to expect and gave Rayleen advice in detail, knowing that Abe and Doug were doing the same with Riley. "Our guys will be around over the next few days as will Don's and Peter's. You won't see them but they will be close to you. I understand that the men on Richard's team will be with Riley and these two ladies will be with you."

"That's right, Rayleen. It's how we do it." Silver tilted her head as she heard a raised voice for a moment. "Riley is protesting that. But we need to keep you two safe. At night, Andrew assures us that there will be off duty officers around your home. We just ask that you don't go out without alerting someone that you are and wait for someone to go with you. Now is not the time to decide to flee. You'll not make it, Rayleen. That's what we're hearing from the streets."

"I know. I spoke with someone from the streets late last night." Rayleen had made contact with an undercover officer who had detailed exactly what she and Riley were facing. "I don't like it but we need to do that." She looked up as Riley dropped down to sit at her feet. "Riley?"

"I know, Rayleen. I know. We have to have someone with us. That doesn't mean that I have to like it." Riley looked up as the ladies laughed before he gave a small grin. "You all said that, didn't you, at some point?"

"We did, Riley." Naomi spoke up, watching the man whom she thought of as a brother. "It's had at this point. You want to break free and run or else find the person and confront them. That can't happen."

"I know. It doesn't mean that I can't dream about it." Riley grew silent, not hearing the conversation among the ladies that had shifted to other topics. He rose to his feet, walking away, needing to find Abe, Don, Peter, and Richard. He had plans that he wanted to make and he needed those men to aid him in that. He turned for a moment to study Rayleen, seeing the beam of sunshine that was streaming across her face. All he could do was pray for her.

Chapter 37

Three days later, Rayleen had had enough of being kept hidden. Riley had asked her to meet him for lunch at Ev's diner and she had readily agreed. She was pacing that way now, having walked down that way. She knew that she had security team members around her and that they were likely dismayed and upset with her for walking. Rayleen needed that. She needed to take back her life and this was one way to do that.

Riley watched her walk towards him. Jostled by the crowd around him, he didn't move and simply waited for his lady to walk to him and into his hug. He looked down at her, a frown on his face. Something had changed but he had no idea what.

"Rayleen?" Riley's voice was soft as he spoke her name.

"Riley? I don't think that we're going to be going in the diner." She stepped back from him as her arm was grasped in a hard manner. "I think this gentleman wants us to go with him."

Riley stared at the man, his heart sinking. Bill had showed him the man's photo the night before and severely warned him about avoiding him. He was a hired assassin. Bill didn't want to explain to his parents and brother what had happened to him.

"I don't know that we will be." Riley could see his brother's team behind the man. "I think instead that this man will be going with the officers who are approaching him." Riley reached for Rayleen's hand, drawing her away from the man even as officers approached and handcuffed him. He simply walked into Ev's diner and through it to her office. That was not the first time that he had done that but it was the first time that he had fled there to save his life and the life of his lady.

Andrew looked up at them. He had a rare day off during the week and had shown up at his aunt's diner with his little daughter, Lia. He frowned for a moment before he realized that Riley and Rayleen were there for a reason.

"Escaping?" Andrew gave a brief grim smile.

"We are. Your team has it under control." Rayleen was grumpy. "All I wanted to do was meet Riley for a meal. Can't we even do that?"

"You can." Ev placed their food orders in front of them. "Eat and then we talk. I have news for you, Riley and Rayleen. Andrew, stay put. You need to hear it as well. Where's Bill?"

"He'll be here now that this has happened." Andrew smiled down as his daughter as she hugged him and then slipped from his knee to climb up on Rayleen's. She didn't think twice about that, just assuming that everyone would let her.

Rayleen stared down at the little girl before she was hugging her and then chatting with her, not quite sure what all Lia was saying but just enjoying the little one. Riley watched her, wishing that it was their daughter. A vision of that crept through his mind and he smiled, not seeing Andrew's intent gaze focused on him..

That afternoon, Rayleen stood back from her front door, watching as Bill approached. His face was grim, she could tell. She sighed. There was no way that she was hiding away with a security team. That was not her. She would run and hide first. Only thing was that if she did? Riley would run right after her. Rayleen would have to plan well if she wanted to hide from Riley as well.

"Bill?" Rayleen's voice brought Bill's head up and he smiled at her. Pointing to the front porch chairs, he waited for her to sit before he handed over the paper cup of coffee that he had for her.

"Here. I needed one and a chance just to sit. How are you today?" Bill grinned for a moment as she glared at him. "Good. Your emotions are still at work. I heard what happened today. That man is not talking but he will be sent elsewhere to face murder charges. God was watching out for you today, Rayleen."

"Yeah and about four security teams as well. I want my freedom and life back, Bill. How close are we to that?"

"We are getting close, Rayleen. As I speak, Jason and Lily are working on arrest and search warrants. We are starting the process of working from the bottom of the chain up." Bill sipped at his coffee, lost in thought for a moment before he prayed for the lady watching him. "This is where it gets dangerous for you both. We still don't have a clear idea why but we know who."

"And you're not telling me, are you?" Rayleen sighed. "I'm sorry. I know that you can't. Not yet. But if I don't know, how to I avoid him or her?"

"It is interesting that you mention a female. They can be more brutal at times than a man."

"That's because we read. And what we read sometimes comes out in real life. People forget that books are not real life and act out the plot lines. And this is exactly what it feels like." Rayleen's attention was on the front lawn, a frown on her face as she tried to determine just who was after her. "Do we have any sense of why?"

"We're getting that, Rayleen. Riley seems to have been incidental to it all. They were after him but were content to wait. When he showed up at the store? That changed it." Bill watched as Riley simply sat beside his lady on the white wicker love seat and wrapped her close to him. "Riley? Any thoughts?"

"Plenty. Most of them I don't like. I know who it is." Riley named a couple, seeing Bill's slight nod. "That's who's after Rayleen and me. I just want to know why."

"And it will come out. You're okay after this morning?" Bill was worried about his friend.

"I am, Bill. I am. I had no real fear this morning for myself. I knew that God is in control. In fact, his angel was standing between Rayleen and that man. She would not have been harmed." Riley was confident in what he had seen and in his words.

"I felt him." Rayleen's voice was barely audible. "I felt him touch me arm and release it from that man's grip. God was there and protected us, Bill. He will not let harm or hurt come to us that He has not already planned for."

Bill was nodding. He knew what she meant. He and Cora had faced the same. Only they had not felt God's presence in the way that this couple was.

Their talk turned to other topics, including the messages that Silas was presenting. Silas had been in touch with each of the couple that day, just to pray with them. They had been grateful for that.

"We have a wonderful friends' group, Bill. We have been through so much but it has only drawn us closer to God." Riley's arm tightened around his lady love.

"We have. It has taken a lot from us and almost driven some of us away from God. But He has been faithful to us." Bill rose at last, his eyes on the keys that he was holding in his hand. "I don't need to say this but I will. You need to be alert wherever you are, even at home. I know that the teams will be around you but life has proven that the bad guys as you call them can still get to you. I don't want to investigate your murders." He walked away, leaving the couple to stare at him before looking at one another.

"He's right, you know. He is so right." Riley's head was resting against Rayleen. "I love you, sweetheart. I don't want to lose you."

"I love you, too. Our lives are in God's hands, Riley. He knows the length of days that we have. I am walking forward without fear, knowing that God will protect. If He chooses, then He welcomes me home."

Chapter 38

Early that evening, Rayleen stood in her kitchen, horror and terror on her face as her hands covered her mouth to still her scream. She watched in disbelief and fear as Riley collapsed almost in slow motion to the vinyl flooring, crumpling to the floor to lie still. His outstretched arm seemed to bounce before it was still, curled above his head. Bright red blood bubbled around the stab wound in his upper chest, to trickle over his body and then to drop almost in a painstakingly slow manner to land in equally bright red bubbles on the floor.

Her eyes raised to the man standing over Riley, watching as he wiped his knife on Riley's shirt before he shoved it into the sheath on his belt. His cruel eyes seemed to mock her. Rayleen knew that a man stood behind her. Her arm was caught in his hard, tight grasp.

Hearing footsteps, Rayleen looked up, her heart seeming to stutter in her chest as she saw who had appeared. It could not be him! She watched the evilness and cruelty that showed on his and the death and depravity shining in his eyes.

"You? Why?" Rayleen's words were torn from her.

"Why? Because of you." Ernest Laing stood in front of her, sneering at her fear. "You are the reason."

"But I don't understand. Why me? I don't know you other than to see you around town." Rayleen tried to free her arm from the man's grip but was unable to.

"You are the reason. Your father owed me big time. When you were twelve, he promised that I would be your husband. He has never fulfilled that promise." Laing's hand raised and then dropped as a puzzled look briefly crossed his face. He just could not lay a hand on Rayleen and he had no idea why. He had never had that problem in the past.

Rayleen recoiled from him in even deeper horror. She knew her father had a cruel streak now but had never expected it to involve her in such a manner.

"I don't believe you. Where's the proof?" Rayleen was challenging him, knowing that it might well mean her death.

"I have it locked away in my office. It's too bad that he had to get himself arrested. You will be leaving with me. You don't have any choice in the matter." Laing stared at Rayleen as she drew herself upright and seemed to change in front of him. He no longer sensed fear coming from her.

"I don't think so. God will never allow it." Rayleen felt herself hauled backwards in a hard manner and then pulled out of the back door. She fought the man, her hands and feet flying as best as she could to free herself. A lucky blow from her free hand slashed across his eyes, momentarily blinding him.

The man's hand slammed into Rayleen's face, knocking her senseless and then to the ground. He rubbed at his eyes, trying hard to focus but not quite able to. He didn't hear the running footsteps that approached the two.

Richard had appeared just moments early, his team in tow. He had had a sudden sense of terror and fear for Riley and Rayleen. The team had just finished work for the day but had willingly followed Richard. Richard had headed for the front door before he paused and then ran around the house. Silver was at his heels. He slid to a brief halt as he saw the altercation between Rayleen and her captor before he launched himself forward, his feet almost not touching the ground. Silver had followed, surprise on her face at the vicious way that Richard had responded. She has never seen that side of her boss before.

Richard's hard, knotted fist connected with the man's jaw, sending him to the grass. He didn't move. Richard then turned to Rayleen, gathering her into his arms. He felt her arms around his neck before he was running for the end of the house and rounding it to find Jason and two officers heading his way.

"Richard?" Jason paused briefly as Richard approached him.

"There's a man on the ground. Silver's there. I need to get Rayleen to aid." He was gone before Jason could ask another question.

Heading for Silver, Jason listened in shock as she described how Richard had reacted. He too had not expected that kind of response but in retrospect, he decided that they should have. Richard and his family and team had been through enough over the past months.

Richard slid to a stop by the waiting ambulance, reaching to gently deposit Rayleen on the stretcher. He then stood, his body angled to watch her and also around her. He could see his team moving around, other than Silver, staying out of the way of the responding officers. Lily stood nearby, ready to take Rayleen's statement.

"Richard?" Lily's voice brought his attention to her. "What do you know?"

"What do I know?" Richard bit out his words, his anger palpable. "Rayleen is down and hurt. I have no idea where Riley is or if he is even alive. Rayleen kept muttering that he was dead." Richard kept a tight control on his emotions but he still worried about his younger brother. All he could do was pray that Rayleen was wrong.

Yells and shouts from inside the cottage brought everyone's attention there. Richard's team looked that way before they were once more monitoring the crowd gathering around them. Silver had appeared, briefly touching Richard's arm before she was in work mode and with her team mates.

The sound of gunfire broke through the early evening air, unexpected as it was. Everyone who wasn't used to the sound jumped. Those who were used to gunfire tightened their grip on their weapons, uncertainty in the air.

Five minutes later, Bill appeared at the door, beckoning for paramedics. They rushed towards him, not knowing what they would find but intent on saving whoever it was that needed saving.

Richard's thoughts turned to the men and women inside. He couldn't not pray for them even when he didn't know who had been harmed. It was not in his nature to ignore that.

Bill walked his way at last, nodding as Jason headed into the house. He paused, his face raised to the rays of the setting sun. It was not good, what had happened inside. He needed to find Rayleen and Richard.

Richard moved slightly away from the ambulance, his eyes on Rayleen for a moment. She was finally still. He could sense that she had begun to give up and that saddened him. He turned as he felt a hand on his shoulder. Bill stood beside him, the stress from the last moments on his face. He was praying for his friend, knowing that he had to inform him that Riley was still alive but hurt.

"Bill? Riley?" There was hope as well as fear in Richard's voice, a combination not usual for him but this was an unusual situation.

"Riley's alive. There's a lot of blood but the paramedics are dealing with it. He looks worse than he is. He's awake and talking. He is also wanting to get up to find his lady." Bill looked past him as the ambulance carrying Rayleen moved away.

Richard's eyes slid closed as he struggled with his emotions. Thank you, God, was all he could pray.

"He's transporting soon?"

"He is. First, I need your statement on what happened when you got here." Bill wrote rapidly as he kept an eye on Richard and then on Riley as he was moved to a stretcher and then the ambulance left. "I'll find you, Richard. Go on and follow your brother." Bill stepped away, his attention on the crowd. They had everyone now, he thought. Or at least he prayed that they did.

Chapter 39

Richard turned to face his parents, hugging both of them before he wrapped an arm around Raleigh. His team and their spouses were there. He could see Silas and Madigan approaching him. He appreciated his pastor and his wife. Andrew and Phoebe had been around as well as had Bill's wife, Cora.

"Richard? What word on Riley?" Rose was highly worried about her youngest son.

"He's with the surgeon right now, Mom. It looked way worse than it is. The surgeon has stated that he can stitch Riley back together without heading to the operating room." He bit at his lip. "It's Rayleen. She was abused by her captor. Her jaw isn't broken, but it is bruised. The thing is that she thinks Riley is dead."

Consternation covered his mother's face before she was away from him and heading for the lady who had her son's heart. She would not be stopped from being with her. Rayleen needed a mother at that point and her own mother just wasn't the one to be there.

Rayleen roused at last, a hand to the ice pack on her face. She looked around, a frown on her face as she realized that she was in the hospital. That couldn't be. On her feet, Rayleen simply walked from the room and searched for Riley. Finding him in the waiting room, she sat beside him, an arm encircling his.

Riley roused as he felt her touch, shaking free his arm and wrapping it around his lady.

"You're okay?" He studied the large purple bruise on her face. "No, you're not."

"I am, Riley. I am. Have they found that man yet?" She looked around as she sensed someone near her. "Bill?"

"We have him, Rayleen. Unfortunately, he won't be answering any questions. He chose to end his life before we could stop him." Bill studied her. "You know why he wanted you."

"I do. It's horrible. I can't even fathom what my father was thinking. He owed that man and promised him when I was twelve that I would marry him. God protected me from that." Rayleen buried her face against Riley, not seeing the anger that crossed both men's faces.

"How does a father do that?" Riley's anger at her father knew no bounds at that point.

"Evil. Greed. Fear. Whatever it takes to get what someone wants." Bill sat back, exhausted as always when a case was solved. "What now for you two? Where are you heading?"

"To Mom and Dad's for the night. John has been in touch. He won't let Rayleen back into the cottage until it has been cleaned. Madigan said that her parents and brother were moving in to clean once you've cleared the place." Riley waited for a moment, not sure if he could even stand. "I still don't understand, Bill."

Bill knew that Riley's family and his team and their spouses had gathered around them. He had received word from Jason and Lily that they had made all the arrests. There was still a lot of work to do in finalizing everything before turning it over to the crown prosecutor but that would come.

"Nor do I." Rayleen looked lost and lonely for a moment.

"Apparently, your father laundered money. We have the proof of that now. He was to do that for Laing but instead of turning the money over to him, he kept it. Over a quarter of a million dollars. He spent it and couldn't repay him. That's when Laing decided that you would be his. And both your parents agreed. That is why your mother is so upset with you, Rayleen. You didn't cooperate with them. Instead you left home and built a life of your own, which now includes Riley."

Bill walked away at last, relieved to some degree that the danger to Riley and Rayleen was over but he was still puzzled that parents could do that to their daughter. He stood for a moment, his face turned up to the night sky, his eyes closed.

"All done, Bill?" Andrew stood beside his friend.

"It is, Andrew. I will never understand the depravity of man. It just seems to be getting worse and worse."

"And it will, Bill, as we come close to when our Lord and Saviour returns. We've talked on that many times." Andrew prayed for his friend and then walked away, heading for home and his own family.

Riley rose at last, with some help from Richard. He tucked Rayleen under his good arm, the other arm in a sling for a few days. He was grateful that she had not been hurt worse but anger that she had been and that he could not have protected her.

"Let it rest, Riley." Richard stood beside his brother late that evening on their parents' back deck. He and Raleigh had chosen to stay overnight as well. "God will avenge. In fact, He has to some degree already."

"I know. It just doesn't make it any easier from a human standpoint. I want to be her avenger." Riley wiped at the tears on his face. His emotions were all over the place.

"I know. I felt the same way. The conference call that we did has helped your lady. And it will help you. You need to find your bed and sleep." Richard's arm rested around his brother's shoulder as he prayed for him. "I can't tell you how scared I was when Rayleen was muttering that you were dead. I am so thankful that you are standing here with me." Richard carefully hugged his brother before moving away. He stopped as he saw Rayleen hesitating behind them before hugging her and praying for her, a hand on her back sending her towards Riley.

Riley turned as he felt a hand on his back and then just swept his lady into his arms. They both wept, their emotions all over the place, but grateful that they were together.

———

Six months later, Riley looked down at the beautiful lady who was his bride. Rayleen and he had married just four weeks prior, not wanting to waste any more time apart. He was more in love with her each day.

Rayleen stared ahead of her towards the gardens. She was already planning what she would do, with Riley's help of course. She was deeper in love with her groom every day. Rayleen had met with her father's side of the family, all of whom had welcomed her back. Her grandparents, in particular, had been overwhelmed with joy to see her again. Rayleen had had no contact with her parents, by her choice, not that they had reached out to her.

"Rayleen? Are you sure you're okay?" Riley asked her that every day, getting the same answer. This time, he was met with a glare even though he could see the smile in her eyes.

"I am, Riley. Just as you are. Now, your parents are expecting us for a meal, did you know that?" Rayleen finally gave in to her laughter.

"I know. You said we'd go, didn't you?" Riley bent to kiss her, hugging her closer to him.

"I did. Your parents have stepped in and become the parents that I always wanted and never had. I thank God for them each day." Rayleen moved away from Riley, reaching for the tiny tuxedo kitten that had somehow found her way into their yard and their lives.

"They love you as a daughter, sweetheart." Riley looked down at the table in the kitchen as they entered. An envelope rested there. They had read the contents and were praying over the request. "What are we to tell Barnabas at the Foundation about this job offer?"

Rayleen leaned against him as she dumped out the envelope again to study the officer. Riley had been offered work as a paralegal dealing with immigrants. It was something that he had dreamed about for years. Rayleen, on the other hand, would continue her work with John.

"You'll be good at this. We don't have to leave our town or our home. Most of your work is done by mail or over the internet. And Barnabas would set up an office for you in their building for when you need to be there." Rayleen looked up at the tall handsome man beside her. "You've made your decision."

"I have or rather we have. I like that they don't give a time frame to answer, that they simply say to pray over it and then reach out with our decision. That's how God works."

"And if you said no, they would just move on. I like that it is a unanimous decision that they come to the board meetings with. Not many boards do that and they should."

"I agree. God has certainly led them over the years, despite what all of them faced." Riley turned as he heard a knock at the door and then headed that way. He took the parcel handed to him, momentary fear in his heart.

"What is that?" Rayleen hesitated to approach him as he set the parcel down.

"I don't know but it's couriered to us by Barnabas." Carefully opening it, Riley stared at the paperwork tumbling out. "How did they know?"

"Know what? That we made a decision? That's what this paperwork it.   It's what we need to complete." Rayleen reached for her phone, sending off a text to Barnabas. She smiled as he sent one back, just welcoming them to the Foundation family. God had spoken to him yesterday that they would come on board.

"God has been so good to us, Rayleen. He has led us through danger and brought us to safety. We will have a story to tell our children if we are so blessed." He bent to kiss his wife before he tucked the paperwork away. "We'll complete this at another time. Right now, my beautiful wife and I have somewhere to be."

Thank you once more for picking up one of my stories, a continuation if you like from other stories, in particularly Richard and Raleigh's. That seems to be how my stories work. My characters cannot stay out of one another's stories. This is never planned. I will be writing one, a character walks in, and then their story has to be told.

God is there wherever we are. He never leaves us. He protects us in ways that we don't know. And my father would agree that there are angels around us, doing God's bidding in just that.

Characters that have appeared in this story are Abe and Emma from *His Guardians*, Bill and Cora from *Hidden in the Hollow*, Silas and Madigan from *Strong Courage*, Doug and Darci from *The Heart of a Lion*, Richard and his team from *His Protectors*, Don and his team from *His Defenders*, and Andrew and Phoebe from *The Potter's Hands*. Lily and Loch are in *Lily*.

May God richly bless each one of you as you walk through this journey called life.

Ronna